A PRESENT OF AN ORANGE

To my beloved Clare, Amy, Guy and Hugh.

A PRESENT OF AN ORANGE

and other stories

SEYMOUR CRESSWELL

COQUETTE PUBLICATIONS

First published in 2018 by
Coquette Publications
Bray
Co. Wicklow
Ireland

Paperback	ISBN: 978 1 78846 051 4
eBook – mobi format	ISBN: 978 1 78846 052 1
eBook – ePub format	ISBN: 978 1 78846 053 8
CreateSpace paperback	ISBN: 978 1 78846 054 5

Produced by Kazoo Independent Publishing Services
222 Beech Park, Lucan, Co. Dublin
www.kazoopublishing.com

Kazoo Independent Publishing Services is not the publisher of this work. All rights and responsibilities pertaining to this work remain with Coquette Publications.

Cover photograph by Michael Stokes
Cover design by Andrew Brown
Printed in the EU

Contents

A Present of an Orange

I was terrified and excited in equal measure. A dream was to come true: I was to spend the night on board *Zephyra* with my father. It was July 1959. I was nine years old, and my parents had granted my wish after weeks of wheedling cajolement.

She lay at anchor in the centre of the estuary at Crosshaven. Her sleek, elegant white hull reflected in dabs and splashes, and her mast was mirrored in a squiggling line across the water towards us. *Zephyra* was a thoroughbred racing yacht that belonged to a wealthy friend of my father's. He rarely sailed but was happy to allow my father and his friends use the boat. They had just won a feeder race from Dun Laoghaire to Crosshaven. It was the opener for the West Cork Regatta, which was to take place over the following week.

My mother had driven my sister and me from Dublin to spend a land-based holiday in west Cork while my father competed in the regatta. Now, at the agreed rendezvous, I stood waiting at the top of the slipway with my mother and my sister as my father chatted and laughed with his crew close to the water's edge. He saw us and made his way up the slip as the rest of the crew dispersed to spend the night ashore. They called greetings to my mother as they passed.

My father saluted my mother with a clumsy, self-conscious kiss. He was awkward about emotion and outward signs of affection. He seemed vaguely embarrassed, but I think he may actually have been pleased to see her. He was never quite sure what to do about my sister and me. He considered parenting to be women's work, and he left all the tender, hands-on stuff to my mother.

'Are you all set then, my boy?' he asked.

'Yes, Dad.'

'You'll take care of him, won't you darling?' said my mother, giving my father a look.

'Oh, he'll be fine. Don't fuss.'

The tide was ebbing in the estuary, exposing flat, muddy reaches below the stony shore. Small seabirds and waders plundered the exposed mudflats for worms and shellfish, working their way methodically along the line of the falling tide.

My father rummaged in the pocket of his jacket and, with a sort of conjurer's flourish, he produced an orange. He wordlessly presented the fruit to me. Presents or treats from my father were unexpected jewels. I stood, marvelling at the gifted orange. Then I heard him calling to me from the end of the slip, 'Come on then!'

I turned to wave goodbye to my mother, and I started to run down the slip. I tripped over a launching trolley and fell heavily, skinning the heels of my hands and my right knee. I dropped the orange and saw it bounce once and roll across the slip, gathering speed before launching itself over the edge to roll again and come to rest on the mud, some distance from the slip. To my shame I started to cry, and my shame increased my tearful misery. My hands and my knee hurt. My dignity was shattered, my pride injured and my orange lost. Against all her usual instincts, my mother took care not to make a fuss and hung back.

'What's up? What's up?' I heard my father's voice as he walked up the slip to where I was sprawled on the sloping concrete. He transferred his cigarette to his lips and reached down to help me to my feet. 'Did you take a tumble?' He produced a handkerchief from his trouser pocket and brushed the grit out of the grazes on my hands with a business-like thoroughness that took no account of my pain. 'Poor old chap.'

'He's lost his orange,' said my mother. 'There it is, on the mud.'

I thought that my father had been about to hug me, a gesture so rare that I can count its occurrence now – a lifetime afterwards – on my fingers. But he did something else instead. Turning from me and my tears, he looked to where my mother was pointing and saw the orange plugged in the mud. He went to the edge of the slip, sat and eased himself down onto the weed-covered stones of the shore, then carefully picked his way across the mud to retrieve the orange. He left a trail of deep footprints in the mud. He squelched his way back to the slip and pulled himself up again, his shoes covered in slimy, foul-smelling ooze. He carefully wiped the orange on the leg of his trousers and handed it to me.

'There you are. Good man!' he said, and he turned and walked down the slip and straight into the water. He marked time in the water as the gloop washed off his shoes, his cigarette all the while dangling from his lower lip, and a clownish grin on his face.

My mother laughed. 'You eejit! You'll never get those dry again!' My mother kissed my cheek. 'Take good care of your father. He's not fit to be allowed out.'

My father was still paddling in his shoes. He untied the little punt and brought it alongside. I sat in the stern while my father took the oars. He rowed us with short easy strokes, quickly and smoothly, to the middle of the estuary where *Zephyra* lay facing upstream into the still ebbing tide. On board he found the first aid kit and administered some Vaseline and Elastoplast to my skinned hands and knee. He then set to the alchemy of priming and lighting the Primus stove on its gimballed mountings. He put the kettle on for tea, which, when it came, was very strong but softened by a slurp of condensed milk from a tin with two holes punched in the top. The cabin was dimly lit by four small porthole windows. It had a special smell: a pleasing mixture of tar, salt, mould and paraffin.

My father made up a bed for me on the port bunk using a rough wool blanket that I recognised from home. 'Are you going to eat that orange?' He held out his hand and took it from me, then opened his penknife and scored the skin in quarters. He handed it back to me, and I peeled it and ate it slowly, sharing segments with my father. It was bittersweet.

I got into my bed. The Elastoplast had come off my knee, and the graze was weeping white plasma and little beads of blood. It stung when it rubbed against the blanket. My hands smelled of orange zest, and my fingers were sticky with juice.

'I have to go ashore for a while now. You'll be fine by yourself, won't you?'

I wasn't sure how to respond to this. I didn't know if this abandonment was part of the arrangement that he had discussed with my mother. But I had to be brave. What else could I do? 'I'll be fine, Dad.'

He lumbered around for a while, organising himself for the trip ashore. 'Now, you must stay in the cabin,' he said. 'You are not allowed to go on deck unless I'm there. Do you hear?'

I nodded.

'Do you want a pee before you settle down?' He led the way up the companionway ladder and both of us stood at the rail in the gathering dusk and peed into the water, shoulder to shoulder. He watched me from the cockpit as I went below again and got back into my bunk. 'No monkey business. Do you hear?' He grinned at me and pulled the sliding hatch closed.

I felt the boat rock as he swung over the side and into the dinghy. I heard the oars splash as he headed for the shore to join the crew in the pub. The sound of the oars drifted back to me, barely audible as the dinghy pulled away. Then I was alone.

I lay in the boat, all by myself in the dark, in the middle of the estuary. My ear was near to the waterline, and I could hear every slap and ripple of the water as it gently caressed the sleek shape of the boat. The air was filled with the sad calls and replies of curlews as they waded in the dusky shallows seeking a late supper – a beautiful sound, but mournful and haunting.

After some time, I began to imagine that the boat had somehow slipped its anchor and was moving downstream, carrying me with it, helpless and alone, towards the open sea. Time passed, and this thought developed into a conviction as I felt the gentle rocking of the boat and heard the lapping tinkle of the water along the hull. I sat up but could see nothing. I knelt, wincing as my sore knee grated on the blanket, but still I could see nothing. Then I stood up on the bunk and peered out the porthole. I let out a cry of fear. The whole view of the estuary shore had changed completely. I could no longer see the slipway and the lights of the road. All I could see were the outlines of trees and bushes, faintly illuminated by a small moon. The boat seemed to be moving fast through the water. I got out of my bunk, climbed the companionway ladder and slid back the hatch. The cold of the dewy night gripped my head and shoulders as, in my panic, I looked in all directions to find out where I was.

I looked over the stern and to my right, where I expected to see the slip head and street lights, but all I could see was fast-moving water which seemed to be carrying me to my death. I scanned to my left and saw, lurchingly stationary, and more or less where I had left them, the calm lights by the slipway, twinkling mockingly at me and winking in a million tiny reflections on the water. Reason interrupted my waking nightmare. As I was drowsing in my bunk, the tide had turned, and the boat had swung 180 degrees on her anchor to face the incoming tide. My heart was racing, but I was safe. Shivering now in the cold, I slid the hatch cover closed. I padded back to the welcoming warmth of my bunk and fell asleep.

I was woken by the sound of the dinghy coming alongside again and the voice of my father calling, '*Zephyra* ahoy! Permission to come on board?' The boat moved under his weight as he swung himself on board and tied the dinghy astern. Then the hatch slid open and a pair of legs descended the steps. My father flicked the last ember of his cigarette over the side before he slid the hatch shut. I saw his face above me, dimly lit by his torch's fading battery. He grinned at me.

'All well?'

'Yes, thanks Dad.'

'We'll say goodnight then. Sleep well.' He settled in his bunk, fully clothed, and pulled his blankets around him. He grunted another gruff 'goodnight' to me and fell asleep. He snored.

I was greatly reassured by the return of my father, but I was also a little resentful that my new floating world had been invaded, just as I had started to feel comfortably in command of it. And I was now kept awake by the snoring of my shipmate. But, eventually, I slept again.

We awoke early. The water was still and mirror-flat around us. Everything on deck was wet with dew. There was no sound except the calling of the seabirds and waders. My father lit a cigarette and the Primus and made bacon and eggs for two.

Brown Boots

I never scored a try – not in four years playing school rugby, trying my best to realise my imagined athletic potential and to emulate the feats of the sporting gods that dwelt on the school's Olympus – but I came close once.

To celebrate my first term at boarding school, my mother answered an advertisement in one of the evening papers and bought me a pair of second-hand rugby boots. These were presented to me with a certain amount of fanfare, and I had to pretend that I was delighted. They were made of thick brown leather and came up right over my ankles. The studs were also made of leather. What I soon discovered was that those boots absorbed moisture like camels at an oasis, and on a wet day they became so heavy that it was nearly impossible to move. I also discovered that brown footwear on the rugby pitch was not in accordance with the accepted dress code. The boots became a magnet for derision and jeering disdain: contumely so readily and joyously poured on the weak by the strong in such a place as boarding school. All the lads who were good at games had new black boots that resembled studded slippers. They were as light as a feather and, to the sulky and begrudging envy of such as me, seemed to enable the wearers to glide effortlessly over the boggy turf to score tries and kick conversions.

I was not very good at sports. I was puny in stature and easily winded. I could not catch a ball; I could not pass a ball. I was a slow and cumbersome runner and was wholly unable to kick a ball more than a foot off the ground. Added to this, I was cautious about getting hurt. So, I was not really First XV material. However, my complete lack of natural ability did not deter my dreams of achieving glory on the field of play. I longed to be able to dash through the opposing defence with gazelle-like grace and speed, to tackle opponents twice my size and to send the ball spinning through the air to bisect the goalposts. I wanted to be the boy who touches down beneath the posts and trots back to his own ranks, stone-faced and heroic. I truly admired the boys who could do these things and, with a remarkable degree of self-delusion, I believed that if I kept at it, I would eventually master the game of rugby. I was convinced that there was an athlete in me, somewhere, struggling to get out.

My best friend, Peter, was even more spectacularly inept at sport than I was. Peter was exceptionally bright academically and led his classes in nearly all subjects. He was a reader and a thinker, but by no means a sportsman. However, instead of pining, like me, for athletic prowess, Peter had a high disdain for all matters to do with sports.

'Useless waste of time, that's what it is,' he would say. 'All sport is stupid, and the idiots who play it are fools.'

'But it's good for us to run around and keep fit,' I would argue, quoting my mother.

'If God had intended us to play rugby, we would have been born with studs on our feet,' replied my brainy friend. 'I really don't know why you are so fixated with it. It's a game for bullocks.'

He did not share my admiration for the school sports stars, who enjoyed godlike status among the rank and file. While I embraced the school ideals of holding a straight bat and engaging in honest and forthright endeavour on and off the sports-field, Peter followed a more personal code, which included avoidance of physical conflict, holding your own against the bastards and surviving till the holidays.

The boarding-school system took no account of ability or preference when it came to sport. Everyone was expected to turn out on the allotted days and get on with whatever activity was prescribed. Two or three times a week during the winter months, usually in pouring rain and bitter wind, I was required to tog out and play rugby, usually with a team of other no-hopers and rejects. I'm not sure what this was intended to achieve, except exhaustion and hypothermia. The pitch that was reserved for our game was steeply sloped from one end and was almost entirely devoid of grass. Even the small and untidy clumps of rushes that decorated that barren wasteland field seemed to struggle apologetically for survival. The coach decided that the position of wing-forward was best suited for my talents, in that I could do least damage in that position and was out of the way. And so, the gruesome business of the training match would kick off, with the coach yelling at me from the start to keep up, to join the ruck, to tackle the opposing team around the knees and generally expose myself to danger. There followed an hour and a half of pointless toiling in a muddy field, sometimes punctuated by explosions of violence inflicted on me by bigger boys if I didn't get out of the way. Even the ball was a weapon. We were expected to play with ancient leather rugby balls that had been kicked around for so long they were no longer oval and had taken on a misshapen roundy form. These balls shared my boots' propensity for the absorption of moisture, and in the slightest shower of rain would rapidly acquire all the bounce and heft of a greasy, ovoid concrete block.

'Catch it! Catch it!' someone cried.

'What, where?' I replied in confusion, staring into the empty, rain-filled sky before turning towards the direction of the voice. Inevitably, I received the heavy ball, which had been kicked with full force by some gargantuan lunatic, smack in the face. It took me some moments to recover my nose and mouth, which seemed to have been smashed into the back of my skull. It was like retrieving the fingers of a rubber glove that had been turned inside out. I refused to resort to tears, but the impact on my nose was so severe that my eyes began to water involuntarily. Blood soon started to flow from my outraged nose and I was honourably discharged from the rest of that games session.

My flirtation with glory happened on a particularly wet and miserable day in March, when we of the Fourth Bs were slogging it out, as usual, on the north face of the sloping pitch. I had been put on the red team for the first half, playing up the hill. At half time I was told to switch, to play for the blue team for the second half, again up the hill. Somewhere in the wilderness of the second half, there developed an endless and directionless sort of rolling maul that resembled a very muddy, many-legged insect, ambling aimlessly across the field. I was hovering around the fringes of this melee, trying to stay out of harm's way, when whoever had the ball seemed to drop it. It came out from under all the legs like a big brown leather egg. I managed to pick it up without fumbling and set off in the direction of the opposing try line. For some reason nobody seemed bothered to chase me, so I continued my laboured run with only the opposing full back between me and glory.

Until this point I had not been aware that my best friend, Peter, was playing in that training match at all, probably because he had been put in as full back to keep him out of trouble, and he had successfully used this to stay away from the focus of play and the distastefully brutal, physical business it entailed. And now, there he was – knees still immaculately clean of mud and shorts still pristine – the opposing team's last line of defence.

Struggling and floundering in the mud as I made my way, ball in hand, up the slope towards the try line, I was gasping for air and my soggy brown boots seemed to get heavier with each stride. The quagmire sucked hungrily at my feet, making each step a Herculean effort. My dream drove me onwards. I was determined to score my first try.

Peter made his way across the pitch in a crab-like sideways motion, his pale skinny legs sticking out absurdly from his clean white shorts. By this time my running had degenerated to a sort of shambling, stumbling fall, with my mud-caked boots barely keeping up with the trajectory of my exhausted body. Despite his unwavering disdain for rugby and his acute awareness of my yearning to score a try, Peter closed in and managed to tangle with me with surprising vigour. All arms and legs, he brought me and my dreams of glory tumbling to earth. I was a yard short of the line.

Afterwards I asked him, not without rancour, 'What did you do that for?'

'It was what I was supposed to do, wasn't it?' he asked, by way of an answer, all insouciance.

'But I would have scored a try.'

'You're the one who thinks it's a good idea to "play the game". What did you expect me to do, let you go?' He was getting quite stroppy now. 'Look, it's not my fault that you weren't quick enough to run around me,' he said, showing a complete and callous lack of sensitivity to my anguished disappointment and a total disregard for my shattered dream.

But he was right. I would have thought less of him if he had not tackled me.

Transmigration

Wilfred Forsythe sailed a large racing dinghy known as a Mermaid. He was actually very skilful and extraordinarily nimble about the boat, in the way that very overweight people are often surprisingly elegant dancers. The boat required a total racing crew of three and Wilfred had his regulars, but sometimes he was short-handed and his circle of friends would be canvassed to provide an able-bodied youngster to fill the gap. He taught many young boys how to sail. Nobody ever questioned the propriety of such one-to-one training and, looking back, that is a good thing because those I know who learned under his careful and patient tutelage recall an entirely benign and knowledgeable instructor. I think I was about fifteen when I was first conscripted to crew for Wilfred. He phoned my father to ask if I could help sail his boat from Dun Laoghaire to Howth in time for the Howth Regatta. For such a passage, the boat was easily manageable by a crew of two.

I was very unwilling to sail with an old man I hardly knew. I could not imagine a less pleasant way to spend a day. The prospect of the endless tedium of such a passage in the company of an elderly and eccentric stranger was horrific. But I didn't have the gall to refuse my father's quiet demand. My shy, self-conscious, adolescent self was not brave enough to deny the request, so I had to find the courage to make myself crew for Wilfred.

He had been a friend of my father's since they were both boys, although Wilfred was a few years older. I don't think they had anything in common except that they both came from the Protestant minority in a small South Dublin community, where virtually everyone knew or knew of everyone else. It is likely that Wilfred's parents and my grandparents were friends and the two boys were forced upon each other, almost like an arranged marriage.

He was rotund and had a round head that was almost entirely bald. His remaining hair was close-cropped. My father said that he looked like the Michelin man. I knew him mostly from seeing him at the sailing club, so he remains enshrined in my memory dressed in a pair of enormous khaki shorts that covered his knees and stretched up and over the generous curve of his belly. They were held in place by a pair of braces and further secured by a brown leather belt. His shirt was invariably checked Viyella which had seen better days. An equally veteran Old Etonian tie was always knotted around the frayed collar. On his feet he wore grey socks with a pair of off-white plimsolls. He was short-sighted and wore wonderfully owlish, round, tortoise-shell spectacles, which seemed to have grown into his face in the way that a wire fence becomes subsumed into the trunk of a tree. Nobody knew what Wilfred did for a living. The unkind said he had never done a day's work in his life, but others said he did something in the stock exchange. He had never married. Perhaps this was owing to shyness. Maybe he was not interested in the opposite sex or the opposite sex found him laughable beyond amorous contemplation. He lived with his unbelievably ancient mother, who was stone deaf.

We set off in the late morning of a fine sunny day, with just enough wind to move the boat along at a reasonable pace so that we might make the best of the tide. It was important that we got around the Baily – the lighthouse at the tip of Howth Head – before the ebb tide set in.

In his carefully modulated delivery, spoken as if he was trying to retain three or four marbles in his mouth, Wilfred quizzed me as to my sailing experience. I had sailed a lot with my father, and it would not have been over-coinage to suggest that I knew the ropes. He was delighted with this and offered me the helm while he sorted out the mackerel lines, which always accompanied him whether racing or pottering.

'I always go for feathers. They look so colourful and dainty, but they get in a fearful tangle, don't you think?'

He carefully unwound the interwoven feathers with their ferocious, half-camouflaged, barbed hooks and almost invisible fishing line from the wooden frame on which they were spooled. A lead weight was attached to the end of the line of six to weigh the rig down as we trolled. I thought about the agonies of the fish as they snatched blindly at the pretty, flickering feathers with their lethal, cruel surprise.

'Feel a bit sorry for the poor old fish, don't you?' said my skipper.

'Yes, Mr Forsythe. I was just thinking the same thing.'

'Call me Wilfred please, if you can. I'm not a headmaster.'

He looked up into the sail and the little flag at the masthead. 'Just bear up a little so that the flood tide doesn't carry us in towards Red Rock.'

I steered, as instructed, out into the bay, with the still distant Baily on our left and the minaret of the new Kish lighthouse on our right.

'Think about a table cloth.' He lowered the lead weight over the side of the boat, allowed the vicious feathered hooks to follow, and then let the stronger, thicker fishing line run off the frame into the sea.

I could not see what a tablecloth had to do with anything, so I didn't respond. Wilfred settled himself on the seat amidships with his back to me, holding the line in his left hand and winding the last of the fishing line around a cleat so that we would not lose the whole rig overboard.

'The sea is like a tablecloth, and we are like a starched napkin folded like a bishop's mitre sitting on the tablecloth.' He gave the line an exploratory tug, auditing for success. 'The tide moves as if to pull the cloth and everything with it, including us in the form of that napkin. The land, of course, is static, like the chairs around the table.'

He fell silent again, generously allowing me to digest this morsel of navigational instruction. The sun warmed my face and reflected in a million sparkles off the gentle sea. The little waves made gurgling sounds as they caressed the hull of the boat. Tiny eddies, like miniature whirlpools, sprung up in our wake. They were decorated by a fine lacework of foam to show the line of the course we had taken. The breeze was coming from over my left shoulder and the sky was a cloudless blue.

Ahead I heard a low moaning sound, intermittent but regular in its way. It was like the sound of an exhausted bullock breathing its last under a poleaxe. I peered under the mainsail to see what was causing the noise. It was a navigational buoy, standing about twelve feet over the water. It had been painted red but was streaked with rust, and the top of it was white with the droppings of many seabirds. In weather-worn white letters were painted the words 'North Burford'.

'A hat of cormorant shit,' said Wilfred. 'How undignified! It marks the northern end of the Burford Bank. If we had a very deep keel, we might be troubled by the bank at low tide.'

The buoy made one of its sighing, groaning noises as the swell lifted it to show a long and straggling beard of brown seaweed clinging to its underside – 'Nguuuh ... Nguuuh', in perfect rhythm with the rise and fall of the waves. To this day I have never seen or heard anything so forlorn and repellent. The thought of it now makes me shudder. It was as if someone had chained a poor animal out in the middle of the bay and abandoned it.

'It has a central cylinder that is fixed to the bottom of the bay and an outer flotation ring that rises and falls with the motion of the waves. The air trapped inside, as the collar is pulled down around the cylinder on the falling wave, is released through a foghorn when the wave drives the collar up again.' He paused and inspected me through his round spectacles, then turned his gaze again to the buoy. 'That's the science, but I sometimes think of it as the soul of some unfortunate who has fallen foul of a particularly nasty god and is condemned to spend eternity in Hades, chained to the bottom of the Stygian sea, almost drowning, almost saved. I always feel sorry for it when I pass it. Mooing there, day and night, without anyone to love it.'

I hadn't a clue where Hades or the Stygian sea were situated, but that didn't harm my appreciation for his description. Astern of us now, the buoy bade us farewell with its pitiful bellow, 'Nguuuh', and I began to see why Wilfred was one of my father's friends. When we had the Baily on our port beam, we let the mainsail swing over to the other side of the boat and altered our course to sail 360 degrees with the tide still under our keel. We had made good time and the tide was still with us. The tablecloth was being pulled northwards, and our mitre-shaped napkin with it, making good progress over the land, past the immovable rocky cliffs of Howth Head. The blue sea broke in white splashing exuberance on the multifaceted black, brown, yellow, grey, pink and green of the ascending headland, capped with the white beacon of the lighthouse.

Wilfred gave a little whoop of delight, 'Aha! There's one for supper!'

He started to pull in the mackerel line, laying it in careful coils on the floor of the boat. There was a flash of silver in the water as the struggling fish was drawn nearer the surface, then was pulled, twisting and fighting for life, into the suffocating air. It dangled for a dripping, writhing moment above the sea, showing the marvel of its beautiful blue-green colouring with its black chevron stripes and silver belly. Its ferocious mouth was agape in awful angry astonishment at the snagging hook. Diamonds of sparkling water flew in the sunlight. Wilfred reached for the fish, grasping it firmly as it shuddered in protest, then with one deft movement he broke the neck of the struggling mackerel and laid it gently in the bucket that served also as a bailer.

'Poor little fellow,' he said as he detached the hook. 'Such a beautiful creature. But so good to eat.'

Ireland's Eye came into view, its form mimicking in miniature the shape of Howth itself. At its north-eastern tip, separated from the island by the narrowest of channels, stood the sharp cragged profile of the Stack, its shape that of a fist with its thumb up. On the rocks, cormorants were standing in sociable groups with their drying wings extended in cruciform. Ahead of us, a hunting party of gannets whirled and circled in the sky before swooping suddenly, swift and dart-like, hitting the water in tiny puffs of white foam to snatch a beak-full of sprat to feed their young.

'The gannets are after the sprat, and so are the mackerel, and we are after the mackerel,' said Wilfred. 'Nature has a strange symmetry, don't you think?'

I wasn't sure what to think. My young brain was astonished at Wilfred's sympathetic interpretation of the beauty of the seascape and the creatures that inhabited it.

'I think it is wonderful,' was the best I could manage, since it seemed that some response was required by my gentle skipper.

'Wonderful indeed. Life is a wonder.'

We were overtaken by a trawler returning to Howth with its hold full of the bounty of the sea – a rusty, battered, blue craft with a stained white wheelhouse. A trawlerman waved to us from the stern as he emptied a bucket of fish-guts over the side. We returned the salute and watched the innumerable gaggle of herring gulls and terns wheel, turn and swoop effortlessly in the slipstream of the trawler, shrieking, squalling and bickering as they vied for the best morsels. The steady, untroubled thud-thud-thud of the boat's diesel engine faded as it pulled ahead, rocking us gently in its wake and showing us the way into Howth Harbour.

The gulls and other seabirds now seemed to be thick in the air above us, hovering and waiting for the fishermen's leavings. Other trawlers were returning to port from the north, each with its squawking halo of avian followers. On the pier, a gull the size of a Christmas turkey observed our passage, its unforgiving amber eyes watching sharply, its savage yellow bill with its downturned tip seeming to sneer at our efforts at navigation. In its immaculate white-and-grey livery, it marched along the wall on its huge yellow feet as if to follow us, occasionally opening its beak to utter its repeated piercing call.

'Do you believe in the transmigration of souls?' asked Wilfred, turning on the seat to look at me. I must have looked very blank because he continued, 'Transmigration. Nice word that. It is the idea that when a creature dies, its soul moves on to take up life in another form. Reincarnation. The Buddhists believe in it. So did Pythagoras.'

Wilfred didn't seem to require a response, so he continued. 'If there is transmigration of souls, when I die please tell them that I would like to be reincarnated as a seagull in Howth.'

Then we were alongside the landing jetty and our voyage was over. I had to excuse myself and make a dash for my train back to Dun Laoghaire. I thanked Wilfred and apologised for rushing away.

'Oh, no. Thank you, dear chap. You are excellent cruising

company. We should do it again sometime. Off you go now and don't miss your train.'

On the train, as it rattled and swayed its way southwards, I thought about the events of the day and found myself astonished by how much I had enjoyed Wilfred's company. I felt honoured that he had trusted me to steer his boat and had shared some of his thoughts on life and death with me.

For whatever reason, I never sailed with Wilfred again. It is hard for a young lad to kindle friendship with an old man without causing misunderstanding. Some years later his mother died and soon afterwards he died too, perhaps of loneliness.

Last year I found myself in Howth again. It was another beautiful day. I bought a ready-wrapped sandwich and strolled over to the new harbour, which was barely recognisable from the tiny port of my memory. There on the quayside stood a huge herring gull, cheekily observing my progress and perhaps hoping I might share my picnic. I wondered if it was the reincarnation of Wilfred, who had lived his life as an unwitting figure of fun, but who was actually so full of kindness and sympathetic understanding. I thought of my father's friend and threw a crust to the seagull.

The Student Prince

The entire school gathered every evening to kneel on the floor of the common room to recite the Rosary. There were subtleties in the manner of delivery of the prayer. Some boys would gradually speed up the responses, while others would slow the tempo to a snail's pace. Without being singled out as the laggard, boys would vie with each other to be the one who would still be on 'now and at the hour of our death' when the rest of the puerile congregation had already sprinted up the home straight and crossed the finishing line with an emphatic 'Amen'.

One evening, shortly after the start of the Michaelmas term, before the Rosary started but after the school was on its knees, the headmaster chose to announce that the school was to mount a production of Sigmund Romberg's *The Student Prince* under the direction of Fr William and the musical baton of Fr Bertrand. The school had never before taken on such an undertaking. The announcement was greeted by silence, followed by murmured expressions of puzzlement and astonished shock. The tension was broken only when the lad whose turn it was to lead the Rosary kicked loudly into the Five Sorrowful Mysteries.

It seemed to me and my good friend Peter that the project displayed a distressing level of naivety among those in charge of things. Peter, who was inquisitively studious, took himself to the library and engaged in some basic research, which showed that the production would require twenty principal players and a chorus of twice that number.

'Of course, you know what's going to happen, don't you?' said Peter. 'They'll cast all the grunters from the top rugby teams. It's what always happens. Then they'll wonder what went wrong.'

'I'm sure that the auditions will be fair.'

'It's all a load of bollocks.'

This was Peter's standard dismissal of all artistic extra-curricular activity.

'Well, I'm going to try for a part.'

'You know you'll be cast as a girl. Your voice hasn't broken.'

My vision of myself as a dashing archduke, in the uniform of a hussar, all frogging and epaulettes, was dashed. I wasn't sure that my first steps to stardom should be taken in a dirndl and a peasant blouse.

'It'll all end in tears. Trust me,' said Peter. 'Besides, I have Bill for English, and he's a complete knob.'

I shrugged. I knew that I would audition anyway.

Fr William was a relatively new arrival in the school, although the rumour was that he had been hiding in the monastery with his hood up for some years. Although he was not a familiar face around the school, he had already acquired the nickname of 'Shrill Bill', a reference to his high tenor voice, which he used to some effect as lead tenor in the monastery choir. He had started his tutorial career only that term, teaching English to the class below me, which included Peter. He had also been appointed choirmaster for the school, and it was there that I had first come across him. He was a tall man with dark brown hair and glasses. He liked to wear his hair sleeked back from his forehead and held in place with some sort of pomade. He had a peculiar way of sweeping into a room, his robes swirling around him, like the villain in a pantomime. He was short-tempered and quick to anger, something of which the boys took full advantage. Angry teachers were considered fair game for goading and pranks.

Nobody seemed to know much about Fr Bertrand. He had materialised from somewhere over the cloister wall, perhaps from one of the sister abbeys in England. He was a short man, standing about five feet two inches in his socks, which were usually a surprising canary yellow. He had wavy, sand-coloured hair that he kept rather longer than was fashionable at that time among the professed monks. He was very red in the face, as if he had been holding his breath. He was rumoured to have a doctorate in music, and it was perhaps this qualification that had singled him out as the maestro for the school production. He was not a teacher in the school, so he was rather hard to pin down, and this meant that his nickname of 'Squirty Bertie' was perhaps a tad lacking in imagination.

We in the choir were introduced to him by Fr William, who gave us to understand that we were under an enormous compliment to have him play the organ for us.

'Quiet, please boys. Quiet. I said QUIET! I would like

to introduce you to Fr Bertrand, who is one of the most accomplished musicians in Ireland. He will be playing the organ for the choir from now on. Quigley, is that chewing-gum?'

'No, Father. I don't know what you mean,' said Quigley as he surreptitiously added his warm wad of Wrigley's to the line of abandoned lumps of gum under the choir stalls.

'Good afternoon, boys. I am very pleased to meet you,' said Fr Bertrand.

His frantically posh, clipped Oxbridge accent caused an immediate stir, but this was quickly overtaken when he rummaged in the pocket of his tunic and produced a tiny silver box, which he held in front of him like a votive offering.

'We will be rehearsing in the chapel from now on so that you can get used to the acoustics and my organ.'

He opened the box and took a pinch of something from it, tapped the lid with a certain ceremony, then stuffed whatever it was up his nose with an ostentatious sniff. To complete the trick, and with a flourish, he then produced a red silk handkerchief from the top pocket of his tunic and noisily blew his nose. The choir was mesmerised as the tiny man wiped his nose fussily and furiously, screwing up his eyes and sniffing vehemently. He looked a bit like one of those Japanese monkeys that hang around hot springs. He held the rapt attention of the entire choir until he had completed his ritual and returned the handkerchief to his pocket.

At choir practice, Shrill Bill would sweep into the chapel in a flurry of robes, smooth back his quiff, whip out a tuning-fork from beneath his scapular, bang it on a pew, hold it to his ear and hum the note. This soon became his signature.

The tuning-fork ritual and the peculiar noise that he made were so easy to mimic. 'Mmnneee!' He would then lead us through the hymn, getting more and more agitated as the tonally challenged among us were unable to pick up our line.

'Are you alto boys deliberately singing the top line?' he threw out rhetorically. 'I've given you your line four times now, and not one of you seems to have picked it up. O'Brien, if you do that once more I'll send you to the headmaster's office. Come on! Trebles and altos only now. Once more.' And he would raise his arms to conduct the farmyard cacophony again.

It took weeks to teach us a basic two-part harmony, and we could feel that the effort was taking its toll on Bill's nerves. He did not hit breaking point, however, until one Sunday night at Benediction, when the choir was in a particularly discordant mood. We had just finished hacking our way through *O Salutaris Hostia* and had administered the 'Amen' by way of *coup de grâce*, when an anonymous chorister offered a loud 'tsshhh', like a cymbal struck to punctuate the end of a pop song. The sound has a particular advantage in that it can be made without moving the lips, leaving its source anonymous.

'Who did that?' came the indignant voice of Shrill Bill, loud enough for the whole school to hear, and effectively drawing attention to the disrespectful sound.

'What, Father? I didn't hear anything.'

'That "tsshhh" noise.'

'There it goes again, Father.'

'Who did it?' Bill was colouring.

'Don't know, Father. Wasn't me. Could we hear the noise again?'

Bill was now beside himself with rage and was in a dither as to whether he should send the whole choir to detention or let the matter go.

'Tsshh!' was volunteered from somewhere in the ranks of the choir. That decided it.

'Right! Two hours' detention for the whole lot of you,' and he stormed out of the chapel, his habit flapping and fluttering around him.

The following day a notice was pinned to the board announcing that auditions for the forthcoming production of *The Student Prince* would start that evening in the gym. Those interested were invited to write their names in the space below. This was signed off by Fr William and Fr Bertrand. As the day wore on, various names appeared in the space, including Bugs Bunny and Al Capone, but by and large the call for volunteers yielded a decent harvest.

At the auditions, nobody from the school choir turned up, although several members had put their names down.

'Where is Dwyer, the tall boy with pimples who thinks he can reach high C?'

'Don't know, Father. I've never heard him.'

'Of course you have heard of him. He's in your class.'

'Never heard him reach top C, I mean.'

'Stop trying to be clever. Where is he, and where is the rest of the choir?'

'In detention, Father.'

'How can they all be in detention when they are needed here?'

'You sent them, Father. You gave them two hours for making a noise. I thought that was what the choir were supposed to do.'

Bill swept out of the gym in a flurry of robes and went in search of the detained choristers.

The auditions took two evenings and would have gone on longer, but it was understood that the headmaster had instructed Bill and Bertie to get a move on. Just about every boy in the school was auditioned. It was more a conscriptive than voluntary exercise.

The school had 150 boys, aged from twelve to nineteen. The hierarchy among the pupils was arranged according to physical prowess on and off the rugby pitch. This system of natural elimination of the meek and talented fed upwards into the school management, so that the boy chosen as head boy was always the captain of the First XV rugby team, and his praetorian guard of senior prefects were invariably drawn from the ranks of that elite team.

It therefore came as no surprise when the cast of *The Student Prince* was announced, that the head boy, Roger Quirke, was cast as Prince Karl Franz, the student prince of the title. This lad was a squat, ugly, dark-haired thug, who played at first centre and was feared throughout Munster for his ferocity on the pitch. He was known to have broken the jaw of an opposing scrum half with a hand-off that would have felled an ox. He was fairly ferocious off the pitch too. He was slightly bandy-legged and enjoyed a particularly florid type of acne. He had an odd, unpleasant, grating voice and a strong Cork accent. He had never been known to sing.

His leading lady, playing the part of Kathie, was a tall, chubby, fresh-faced lad from Tipperary called Pat O'Toole. He had unruly blond curls and no particular talent, unless you count hyperextension. This otherwise unprepossessing boy could join his hands behind his back and, without separating them, bring them over his head to the front. This trick is hard to describe and even harder to watch. He played in the second row on the Junior Cup XV and towered over the prince. Pat's voice was on the squeaky edge of the treble range.

Various other stalwarts of the corrupt school regime – top bullies, Mafia chiefs and hitmen – were slotted into the other parts as the audition process proceeded on its predetermined course. I was consigned to the chorus, where I would be required to perform as a maid-at-court in the court of Karlsberg and as a backing barmaid at the Three Golden Apples. Peter's scorn was withering.

'You probably won't even get your name in the programme. All the principals will be named, and you will be in as "and members of the chorus". Welcome to your fifteen minutes of fame.'

The rehearsals started at the beginning of October. There were difficulties from the start. It emerged that our glorious head boy and rugby captain, Roger, was tone deaf. This ought to have been apparent at the auditions, but Bill and Bertie were blinded and deafened by the glamour associated with the boy's status as prince of the school. It seemed natural to cast him in the leading role, although he sang like an ass in heat and had all the histrionic capabilities of a railway sleeper. His leading lady, Kathie (Pat), had a nice treble voice, but he produced it so quietly that nobody could make out what he was singing. This was compounded by Matron, who was in charge of wardrobe and had produced a blonde wig for Kathie that looked like the ears on a golden cocker spaniel.

'Always sing over a full lung, boy. Breathe from your

stomach and project!' hollered Bill from the back of the gym.

'Sorry Father, what was that?' said Pat, lifting one of his floppy ears. 'I can't hear anything in this wig.'

Then the chorus was herded on stage for the binge song, 'Drink! Drink! Drink!' Peter was delighted to hear of this song and assured me that it would go down a storm with the invited parents. Then we rehearsed the anthem, 'Come, Boys. Let's All Be Gay Boys'. Although at that time the word 'gay' meant something happy and frivolous, there were undercurrents of counter-culture that suggested another meaning altogether, and by the second week of rehearsals the scene with that song had degenerated into an uncontrollable riot.

'Boys in the chorus! Boys in the chorus! Quiet please!' Bill was winding himself up to one of his furies. 'Quiet! I WILL HAVE QUIET!'

'Sorry, Father. We couldn't hear you, Father.'

'One more time,' Bill shouted hoarsely, 'and let's try to do it together: "Let's All Be Gay Boys".'

On cue, Squirty Bertie struck up manfully on the ancient piano that was a full tone below pitch and sounded like something from a Wild West saloon, while the cast of teenage boys giggled like the idiots they were, but could not bring themselves to sing in unison.

The production date was less than a week away, and it was clear to all in the cast that the show would never be ready. It was not a question of shortage of rehearsal time. The show would, simply, never be ready. Nobody knew their words; nobody knew their tunes; nobody knew when to come on stage, what to do when they got there or when to leave.

Then the organ and the costumes arrived. The organ had been hired from a specialist firm in Leeds and arrived in two massive crates on a lorry, with a construction manual the size of a telephone directory. The costumes came from a theatrical costumier in Covent Garden. Squirty Bertie, assisted by Shrill Bill, started to assemble the organ in the gym, while Matron and the school nurse opened up the four enormous wicker hampers of costumes and tried to sort out which costume was meant for whom. There had been a mistake with the shoes, so most of the cast were told to wear tennis shoes.

All the parents had been invited to attend the 'for-one-night-only' gala performance. Invitations had been posted two weeks before the performance date. I had written to my parents urging them in the strongest terms to ignore the invitation and to stay at home.

The headmaster and matron attended the dress rehearsal the night before the performance date. They sat in the unheated gym and watched the horrific debacle unfold, line by prompted line, to the accompaniment of the ancient jangling piano, as the assembly of the organ had gone badly. It was clear that the show was not fit to be aired in front of an audience. The headmaster was seen more than once to shake his head in astonished horror. The final nail was driven into the coffin when, after the first rendition of 'Gaudeamus Igitur' at the end of Act II, the inevitable happened. The chorus had just fumbled and fluffed its way through the song and had brought it to a ragged finish when, from somewhere, came that noise: 'Tsshh!'

The production was cancelled. It was put out that Kathie's voice had broken.

Right of Way

It is a balmy evening in early September 1966, and Nelson has only recently been blown off his pillar. The weather is warm and mild enough for there to be a large number of spectators on the terrace of the yacht club, enjoying the air and watching the end-of-season race.

The end-of-season race is organised so that all the dinghy classes, including junior sailors, participate in a single race inside the harbour. There is a handicap start, so the slower, smaller boats go before the faster boats, and from then on it is a chase to the finish, with the first boat across the finishing line winning the race.

My father is a prize-winning champion helmsman. His boat is called *Coquette*, and she belongs to a very old, in fact the oldest, dinghy class called the Water Wags. There has been a fleet of Water Wags racing in Dun Laoghaire harbour since 1887.

He usually sails with my mother, but on this occasion he has dragooned me into crewing for him. I feel resentful and sulky in the truest traditions of teenage sons when compelled to do anything with their parents. But sulking is wasted on my father, who simply ignores it. He is a mild-mannered man, even-tempered and equable even in a boat. He very rarely uses strong language; 'damn' is about as hot as he gets. Among my peers, my language is adequately scatological and profane – it wouldn't be cool to speak otherwise – but with my father I have to mind my tongue, because, for all my adolescent disdain for him, I don't like to cause offence.

I would like to be able to say that my father taught me how to sail. I would like to be able to say that he passed on all his knowledge to me, and that I have become a skilful racing helmsman under his tutelage. But, alas, my father is not a good teacher. Like a singer with perfect pitch, or a mathematician who dreams in quadratic equations, my father's talent as a sailor is largely intuitive, and he cannot understand why anyone might find the dynamics of sailing the least bit difficult to grasp. Once, when I was crewing for him, and we were on an upwind leg of the race, when boats have to sail a zig-zag course into the wind (known as tacking, or beating to windward), he tacked at a particular moment and overtook four boats. I asked him why he had tacked at that moment.

'Because it was the right thing to do.'

'Yes, but why?'

'Because we gained four places in the race,' he replied with a hint of parental patience in his voice.

'Yes, but what made you tack just at that moment?'

There was a pause as he tried to establish in his mind exactly to what level of imbecility his son had descended.

'Because it was the right thing to do.'

That was all he had by way of tutelage. Sailing is not an

easy sport and, no doubt, my father thought I was not an easy pupil.

At the start of the end-of-season race there is a bewildering fleet of dinghies of different classes and sizes, all milling around the starting line – each boat apparently out of control – and going in different directions. There are warning cries of 'Starboard!' from boats on the starboard tack as they assert their priority over boats on the port tack. There are also other more colourful, less technical, shouts. In this melee, the slightest mistake could mean disqualification because under the rather unforgiving, Old-Testament-style racing rules of the time, a boat that fouls another boat or breaks any of the other rules is automatically debarred from the race.

My father sits, unperturbed, in the bottom of *Coquette*. The sun shines on the many-coloured sails: the blue sails of Enterprises, the red of Mirror dinghies and the off-white of Fireflies and Water Wags. The start line is set over by the East Pier near the bandstand. There is a light breeze from the south-west, which mercifully blows away most of the strains of 'Lara's Theme', plucked with relentless persistence by a busker with a banjo on the pier. The crowd of boats gradually thins out as the slower classes are given their starting signals, and eventually the Water Wags are started, setting off in pursuit of the early starters like predators on the scent of their dinner.

The course is set in a triangle so that the boats have to beat to windward, zig-zagging up the first leg right across the harbour to round the first buoy by the Coal Harbour, ease the sails and bear away to sail in a straight line to round the next buoy, anchored near the West Pier lighthouse. Once around the second buoy, we must run with the wind astern back to the East Pier bandstand for another verse of 'Lara's Theme'. I have heard it said that this banjo virtuoso can play only two tunes, and 'Lara's Theme' clearly isn't either of them. We are to sail around this course four times, then beat to the finish in front of the club.

By the end of the first round, *Coquette* is moving like a greyhound, overtaking slower boats and gradually making her way up the polyglot fleet. On the second beat, as we are sailing fast on the port tack, we encounter another boat on the starboard tack. The other boat yells a warning but my father sails on, apparently on a collision course with the other boat, now hardly twenty yards away. There is more shouting, and I check that my father has seen the danger, but he stays calm and at the last minute executes a flawless tack just under the lee bow of the other boat.

'Now I'll break his heart,' he mutters, while with superb, ruthless skill he persuades *Coquette* to accelerate and sail at a more acute angle to the wind, leaving the other boat behind and almost stationary in the backwind from her sails. My auld fella could be really cool sometimes.

On each leg of the course, *Coquette* continues to gain places and I have forgotten that I don't want to be there. We seem to do especially well on the tricky windward legs. It is as if the continuous strains of 'Lara's Theme' are too much to bear, and the boat goes faster in order to get away from the awful plunking noise of the banjo on the pier. By the time we round the buoy by the bandstand for the last time, we are in the lead. There is only one boat between *Coquette* and the finishing line. We are nearly a full round of the race ahead and are about to lap it; it is not in contention for the prize. It is a Mirror Dinghy steered by an angelic-looking girl of about twelve with blonde hair tied in bunches. My father has the bit firmly between his teeth as he tacks towards the finish. I will the boat onwards with every sinew.

Going for a famous win, with a large gallery of spectators observing from the terrace, we find ourselves sailing for the finishing line on the port tack, with nobody except the little blonde girl in the Mirror to worry about. The courses of the boats converge. The wind has by now gone very light, so both craft are moving slowly and events seem to take place in slow motion. On shore, I can see the race officer readying the little black cannon to fire the winner's salute.

There is a voluntary tradition that racing boats have right of way over cruising boats. My father forgets, in the heat of the moment, that the child in the Mirror is a competitor, albeit a competitor already vanquished. He hails her, 'We're racing. Please let us through!'

There is no response from the little boat with the red sails.

'I say! We're racing. Let us through!'

Then, in a high-pitched soprano, clear enough for all on the terrace to hear, the blonde angel shouts back, 'You can fuck off. I'm on starboard.'

My father is so astonished that he takes evasive action slightly too late, and *Coquette* bumps into the Mirror, extracting a volley of extraordinary oaths from the juvenile skipper, culminating with, 'And you can fuck off home now. You're out of the race.'

And indeed we are.

We have committed a foul. With enormous dignity my

father gathers himself, turns the boat and sails for home. He calmly accepts that he must retire from the race. The race officer stands back from the unfired gun. I think I can hear laughter from the terrace. I am seething with outrage and choking with disappointment. Surely we are not disqualified after all that?

I see my father grinning at me from the cockpit, a Players' Navy Cut in the corner of his mouth.

'Them's the rules. There's no point getting upset. She has quite a gob on her for a child, don't you think?'

And I am in awe of my old man.

Ignorance of the Law

I met Tom at my first lecture in Trinity College Dublin. By chance we were seated together in a lecture theatre in the Museum Building. The room had three huge windows, two opening onto New Square and one onto the podium of the New Library. The ancient fixed benches and desks were deeply carved with names of previous generations of students. Our antecedents seemed to have had very sharp knives and endless undisturbed leisure to have achieved this high level of decorative adornment.

Nobody knew anyone else in the class, so it was a rather awkward gathering. We eyed each other sceptically as we folded our unfamiliar black undergraduate gowns around our shoulders. I decided early that we had been bestowed with an exceptionally nice-looking crop of female students. One or two of these young ladies were very pretty indeed. I heard English accents and the rather over-loud tones of some ex-public schoolboys. There were also accents from Northern Ireland and from across the spectrum of the middle classes of the Republic.

Tom seemed to exude confidence in inverse proportion to

my timidity and inhibition. He was skinny with an unruly mop of black curly hair on top of his narrow face.

'Well I guess we should introduce ourselves. I'm Tom Lannigan,' he said, offering me his hand.

He had that posh, English public-school swagger and assurance that I had noted and envied in some of the others, but he also had an engaging, rather lopsided grin, and I felt my reserve melt a little. I told him my name as I shook his hand. By this time our lecturer had made his entrance and the class had come to order.

'Good morning, ladies and gentlemen. Please keep order while I call the roll.'

He did so in alphabetical order, using only surnames, adding a gallant 'Miss' before the girls' names. He glanced up as each student responded to his or her name. He came to Hosforth-Tanner, a very tall youth in a rust-coloured jacket and a red paisley cravat, who acknowledged his name with a cheery 'Present!'

'I'm sorry, Mr Hosforth-Tanner. I can't see you.'

The student rose from his seat and said, 'But I'm here, Professor Russell. Here, in the second row beside the prettiest girl in the room.'

The girl beside Hosforth-Tanner blushed. He was not exaggerating.

'Without a gown you are improperly dressed, and I cannot see you,' Professor Russell replied.

There was laughter as the gownless Hosforth-Tanner subsided and the pretty girl smiled in a sort of triumph.

'Ladies and gentlemen,' continued Professor Russell, 'there are seventy-two of you including the invisible Mr

Hosforth-Tanner. I beg of you to take careful note of the person sitting on your left and the person sitting on your right. Have a good look at them please. Remember them, because they will not be here this time next year.'

With this chilling prediction, Professor Russell initiated our career as students of law. After this first lecture, Tom suggested that we have a cup of coffee in the Buttery, the Trinity canteen, coffee shop and bar. I was not used to such easy acceptance, such casual engagement of friendship. I was more used to an elaborate and cautious choreography before sticking my head above my self-protective sandbags. But here was this engaging stranger, all confidence and charm, extending an offer of friendship to me, and it seemed churlish to refuse. We stepped our way across the cobbles of Front Square and down into the cellars of the Buttery.

Tom told me that he lived in County Wicklow and had been at boarding school at Stoneyhurst in England, one of the grandest Catholic public schools and run by the Jesuits. I asked him what he did about transport, living so far from the centre of Dublin.

'My parents felt sorry for me, living so far out, so they bought me a Fiat Bambino,' he said apologetically. 'I call her Lolita. She's red and has a sunroof.'

I had worked the previous summer as a film extra on a completely forgettable movie, and my wages allowed me to buy a small, noisy motorbike. Each day of that first term I commuted from my parents' home in Dalkey on my motorbike, to and from Trinity. I never had any spare money, so much of my time between lectures was spent in the library, diligently following up on the leads given to us by our lecturers.

The Law School had idiotically offered us constitutional law as part of the first-year curriculum. None of us knew what on earth constitutional law was supposed to be about. An earnest girl in the front row asked our lecturer, Professor Eldon Y. Exshaw, to enlighten us.

'Constitutional law is, of course, the law relating to the Constitution,' he said in his constipated nasal monotone.

Professor Exshaw preferred to smoke a pipe, and he wore a black homburg and a long black woollen overcoat. He looked for all the world like a perambulating black snowman. Exshaw had a peculiar way of lecturing. He intoned his words in a tuneless chant without seeming to pause for breath and without any effort to introduce light and shade, intelligence, inflection or passion into any part of the subject matter. We discovered very soon that he was reading from notes that had been prepared by a predecessor, and his rendition of the other academic's notes was delivered in his somnolent drone at a pace that was just too fast for dictation and just too slow to be remotely interesting. Attendance at his lectures fell rapidly, and soon the numbers were down to single figures. Undeterred, Professor Exshaw continued to plough through the entire roll call before each lecture as if he had been programmed to do so, or, even more likely, as if he was so intellectually stultified that he could think of no other way of starting a class. As he lectured, his stuffed, regurgitated wisdom on constitutional law would be allowed to build up a head of steam and then he would draw it to an agonised conclusion with the grand phrase that was his hallmark and banner:

'*Consequently therefore*, it can be seen that Eamon de

Valera's attachment both politically and religiously to the Roman Catholic faith had a profound bearing on the Constitution of 1937.'

The rate of attrition was mounting among the freshman law students.

*

That summer, one of our classmates, Robert Birch, invited a group of us to his parents' house in Essex for a week. Tom offered to drive in Lolita, with me as passenger. The night before our departure on the Holyhead car-ferry, Tom spent the night at my parents' house. When the four of us sat down to dinner in the family kitchen, my mother chatted cheerily to Tom during the meal while my father maintained his usual reserve. I nervously tried to navigate the conversation through the icebergs of my father's bounteous disapproval. The subject of 'mixed' marriages came up, and my mother told Tom that the archbishop would not allow such marriages to take place at the altar in a Catholic church, decreeing that the ceremony could take place only in the seclusion of the sacristy, lest the god-fearing holy Catholic congregation might be scandalised by the public blessing of the unholy match. She explained that, for this reason, she and my father had gone to London for their wedding, where this stupid bigotry did not apply.

Very early the next morning we departed on the car-ferry to Holyhead, crossed the Irish Sea and rattled our way down the motorway to London. We stopped for a sandwich and coffee at a motorway service station.

'Two coffees, please. One white and one black, please.'

'You mean one wiv and one wivout, love,' said the bored

lady at the till. It was my first introduction to the world of racial political correctness.

A Fiat Bambino has a very small engine, which is seated at the back of the car. The reverberation of that little engine continued in my bones for nearly a day after we arrived in Essex. I can still remember the sound of the engine at full stretch for mile after mile of road and the peculiar humming sensation that lingered long after the journey's end.

Robert's parents lived in a wonderful half-timbered house on the main street of an ancient village. The oak frames of the house had been slotted together sometime around 1540 and had held together ever since. Each room had its own special topography, with undulating floors, crooked, idiosyncratic walls and low unexpected beams. The leaded windows admitted a delicious light, reflecting in dazzling radiance from the wooden floors that shone with the patina of 400 years of domestic service. Although the house was not big, its geography was bewildering. To get to the room that Tom and I were to share, we ascended a tight twisted stairway, went along a short passage and down some more stairs, turning sharply to our left, so that it seemed to me that we were winding our way into a spiral. Robert pushed open the lovely ancient oak-planked door and showed us into our room, adding a 'mind your heads' just a half-second behind the game as we each in turn smacked our heads against a charming fifteenth-century oak beam that ambushed us upon entry. We took to manoeuvring in a semi-crouch as we unpacked our bags.

Two girls from our year and Robert's girlfriend, a first-year engineering student, had arrived ahead of us by plane and train. One of the girls was the very pretty one who had sat beside the invisible Hosforth-Tanner. She was Louisa, and she was Tom's girl.

'Isn't she beautiful? Isn't she a cracker though, don't you think?' And with a pause too narrow for interjection, contradiction or affirmation, he added, 'God, I think she's lovely!'

My pal was in love.

Robert Birch was a slightly flamboyant youth, given to wearing his trousers at half-mast, so that his rather flat feet, shod in Hush Puppies, looked as if they had been attached to the ends of his legs as an afterthought. He wore his thin, very straight hair parted in the middle, and he smoked his cigarettes in a strange backwards style, in the manner of an exiled Russian lower-order aristocrat. He liked to wear his overcoat over his shoulders like a cloak. He was absurdly well-read and was very knowledgeable about classical music. By comparison, I was a yokel, but Robert took kindly care not to flaunt his precocity at us and seemed happy in our company. Together we visited the local stately home and admired its collection of paintings. Robert's mother drove us to Brighton, where we ate candyfloss and spun on the centrifuge of the Waltzer until we all felt sick.

Tom took especially gallant care of Louisa. I felt a little excluded and tried to suppress my resentment of Louisa's intrusion into my friendship with Tom. But she had a charm about her and won me over easily when, one day, Tom insisted on giving her a lift in his car and she said that I must come too. She seemed to understand my attachment to Tom and was not bothered by it.

Robert was an only child, something he held in common with Tom. He had also been at public school, so he and Tom seemed to have a lingua franca in which I was only partly fluent. English terms of art were different from their Irish equivalent: to me a fag was a cigarette, for example. His father had, in recent years, energetically converted to Catholicism, while his mother clung to the Anglican tradition and retreated into deafness. Dinner was quite a formal ritual, with Mr Birch at the head of the table and the rest of us assembled in some sort of order on either side, with poor deaf Mrs Birch smiling bravely at the other end.

The conversation, orchestrated and conducted by Mr Birch, was esoteric and rarefied. If one of us confused Titian with Rubens or muddled the writings of a Brontë or two, we were frowned upon with some severity from the top of the table. Disapproval of innocent ignorance is rather futile and very condescending, and it resulted in a strong feeling of discontentment among the guests.

Robert's engineering girlfriend, by way of conversation at that dizzy Olympian level, said that she had listened to, and enjoyed, her father's record of *Carmen* featuring Maria Callas.

'I consider Maria Callas to be vulgar and unacceptable. Her voice is coarse and simply doesn't compare to the vocal tones of Sutherland,' announced the head of the household.

We had visited an outdoor exhibition of sculpture that day and had seen some fine pieces by Henry Moore. Tom remarked how wonderful the large bronze *Mother and Child* looked with the raindrops streaming down its curves.

'Moore is a pornographer and his sculpture is of no worth,' pronounced Mr Birch.

After dinner, to my intense surprise, Mr Birch decided that it would be amusing to recite racy Limericks:

> There was a young lady called Alice
>
> Who pissed in the Vatican palace.
>
> It wasn't the need that prompted the deed
>
> But sheer bloody Protestant malice.

I was halfway into some sort of replying salvo, featuring Joseph and Mary trying to decide what to call their new infant, when I was brought up short by Mr Birch.

'No, please don't go on. I know this one and it is blasphemous. I would rather not hear it at this table if you please.'

I shrank into excruciated dumbness, and coffee was accompanied by a tense silence, broken only by the tinkle of apostle spoons on bone china. Tom caught my eye and winked. Afterwards Robert privately apologised.

'Sorry about my father. He feels the need to dominate. Bit of a prat actually.'

In our shared room, Tom's endorsement of Robert's view of his father was emphatically stated: 'Jesus, what a wanker!'

At the end of the week, Tom drove to London with Louisa in his little red car, with its sunroof open, to meet her parents. I voyaged home by bus, train and ferry. By this time, I had become accustomed to Louisa being part of my friendship with Tom.

*

The following year, Tom announced that he was going to rent a flat for a fortnight in the centre of Dublin in the run-up to our mid-year exams. He asked if I would share with him. Somehow, I managed to persuade my parents to pay my share of the rent.

The flat was on the third floor of a building on South Anne Street. A toy shop had once occupied the ground floor, but this had long since closed down and the shop space was vacant and full of dusty lumber. The hallway was cramped and dark. It was painted chocolate brown and showed a dirty cream where it was chipped or scratched. Garlands of cobwebbed wires festooned the walls, looping and trailing towards a fuse box high above the boarded-up door to the defunct shop. Steep, narrow stairs were covered in battered linoleum. There was a tilt to the old building that could be felt as you climbed.

The accommodation was a bed-sitting room with separate beds, a makeshift kitchen and a sink that doubled as a washbasin. Ancient porridge-patterned wallpaper covered the walls, frankly showing the stress of its years in its dark blotches, mysterious stains, bulges and peeling cobwebbed corners. A communal lavatory was down two flights of stairs. The furniture had all seen better days, and there was a general odour of unwashed clothes, damp and mice. It was heaven.

Tom had made all the letting arrangements with a Mr Semple, whom we understood to be a bass player in a rock band while studying philosophy in Trinity in his spare time. The rent was paid to Mr Semple in advance and we moved in.

I was a rather diligent student. The fear of failure pushed me towards the library and its amassed learning and actually made me open the prescribed texts, which I attempted to read and understand. I remember, in particular, a book on private Roman law by a scholar called Leage (now, happily, out of print). I read that book from cover to cover without understanding or absorbing a single word within its pages. I remember nothing of the contents of this book, and I doubt whether mastery of private Roman law could possibly have made a better lawyer of me, but it was on the curriculum and I convinced myself that I was at least one step ahead of disaster.

On the evening of our second day in our new quarters, there was a knock on our door. Tom opened it and there stood a small woman aged about sixty, with wispy greying-brown hair done up in a semi-disentangled bun. She wore an ancient floral-pattern dress, elasticated stockings and bedroom slippers. She advanced into the room cautiously.

'Good evening,' said Tom. 'We are subletting from Mr Semple.'

'Well, nobody told me,' she said, with a slight querulousness in her tone.

'Oh dear. Are you the landlord?' I asked.

'No, no, no. My name is Miss Anne Fitzgerald. I live downstairs, but I sort of keep an eye on things. You see you can never be too careful.' She looked around the room as if doing a mental inventory of the fixtures and fittings. 'Will you gentlemen be staying long?'

We explained that we were staying only for two weeks in the run-up to our exams.

'Oh, and what are yous studying?'

'We are second-year law students at Trinity,' I said. It always sounded good: intellectually and societally worthy.

'Oh, law students. Yes. Of course the judges are all part of it, you know,' said our visitor.

'Part of what, Miss Fitzgerald?'

'They are part of the organisation that is taking over the world. There's thirteen leaders and they are taking over everything. Medicine, law, politics – everything. Satan is at the head of the group. It is all his doing. It all starts with the fluoridation of the water, you know.'

'Does it really?'

'Oh yes. Fluoridation of the water is the first step. They put fluoride in the water so that they can control your mind. Governments don't understand it. Governments think that fluoride is good for your teeth, but it is the instrument of Satan. They shouldn't be let away with it. They will take control of your mind. It starts with a tingling of the feet, you know.'

She stood in the middle of the room, her bird-like hands restlessly massaging each other as she moved from foot to foot.

'The head of the biggest food production company in the United States of America is one of the thirteen. He is slowly poisoning the whole of America. The trademark for that company has thirteen stars and three sixes. That's the Devil's number. Only for the Pope and our holy bishops in Ireland, we would be taken over here too. The president of Russia is another member of the thirteen. He's a devil worshipper. May Jesus and all the saints in heaven protect us. Well, goodnight, gentlemen.'

Without another word she turned and shuffled out the door in her slippers.

About a week later, well after midnight, Tom and I were woken by the sound of a key in the lock of the door. The light was switched on. I heard a female voice say, 'Oh my God! What the hell?'

'Hello. Can we help you?'

'What are you doing in my flat?' asked the intruder.

She was a few years older than Tom and me. She wore a long black cardigan and an Afghan sleeveless jerkin, a black skirt that reached the floor and a black floppy hat. There were traces of feathers, lint and loose hairs stuck to her clothes. She took off her hat. Her longish dirty-blonde hair was held off her face by a clasp. Her face was pale and she wore no make-up. She had small eyes and rather heavy pale lips.

'We are subletting from Mr Semple,' Tom explained from his bed.

'That bastard! He has no right to sublet anything. This is my flat.'

'Sorry, we didn't know that.'

'Well, where the fuck am I going to sleep?'

Her accent was English middle class. It made the swearword sound quite exotic.

Tom and I remained sitting up in our beds, sleepily observing our new visitor, unable to think what to say to her.

'I'm Liz, by the way. That fucker Semple is my ex, and he has no right to sublet, but here you are.' She paused, picked up her suitcase and swung it up onto the end of my bed. 'I'll doss with you head to toe,' she said, as if that sort of sleeping arrangement was normal in her life.

Wild half-formed sexual fantasies started to whirl around in my head. The thoughts of sharing my bed with this posh English girl who dressed like a hippie and swore like a man sparked off all sorts of fervent pornographic imaginings in my callow brain.

Liz had just kicked off her shoes when there was a voice from behind her.

'What's going on here?' It was Miss Anne Fitzgerald in her dressing gown and slippers. Her hair was in a hairnet.

'Oh, hi there, Miss Fitzgerald,' said Liz. 'Didn't mean to disturb you. I wasn't expecting sub-tenants in my flat tonight. I was going to sleep top to tail with one of them. We'll sort it all out in the morning.'

In the midst of my fermenting imaginings, I paused, doubtful. She had said 'one of them'. One of them? I had clearly understood that I was the one to share with her; it had been settled. Was she switching allegiance to Tom? Besides, he still had Louisa.

'You'll do no such thing,' said Miss Fitzgerald firmly. 'Not under this roof. You'll spend the night with me, so you will.' She stood in the doorway, arms folded, with a determined look on her face.

'Oh, OK. If you're sure it's no trouble,' said Liz, giving in with an easy compliance that casually dashed my overheated hopes and dreams. She lifted her suitcase off my bed and made her way out the door.

'Goodnight, gentlemen,' said Miss Fitzgerald primly, and she switched off the light and closed the door with the air of a school matron who had successfully interrupted a midnight feast.

I fell asleep wondering how things had got along between Liz and Mr Semple when he was still in favour, with Miss Anne Fitzgerald as chaperone.

We left the next day. Somehow we passed that exam. It was a close thing.

*

Professor Russell's prediction was gruesomely accurate. Only thirteen of the original seventy-two of us lasted the full course of four years' legal studies. Tom, Louisa and I were of that obdurate number. My survival was more due to stubbornness than to intellect or academic ability. Other far brighter brains (including Robert Birch) couldn't stand the stress and tedium of it and migrated to other, more stimulating courses. Some dropped out of college altogether, broken on the stultifying wheel of legal studies. Robert drifted away from our circle, finding new, more scholarly comrades. Of the thirteen survivors, only two went on to practise as lawyers. Tom was not one of them. He married Louisa soon after leaving college and they moved to England, where he worked as a librarian and she worked in the social services.

Years passed and we lost touch except for an annual Christmas card, nearly always in Louisa's distinctive round hand. Forty years later, unexpectedly, Tom phoned me to ask for a bed for a night. He explained that a cousin had died and he wanted to attend the funeral. Of course I agreed.

I waited in my car for him to arrive on the Air-Coach from the airport. It was a cold spring day, but the sun was making a brave effort to gain possession of the skies, and it shone brightly between the showers. I had kept the wipers on intermittent, so my vision through the windshield would become rain-spotted and blurred, then clear as the wipers gave their timed swipe. The screen was partly obscured by rain when I saw a slightly stooped figure step off the bus, dragging a wheeled cabin bag. He looked around him then stopped by the bus stop. The wipers cleared the screen and I recognised Tom. In so many ways, he was still the same jaunty, skinny lad I had known all those years ago, and yet he had aged in a savage way. His hair was grey and thinner than I remembered, and the lines and wrinkles on his face seemed to be deeper than the weathering of years. I wondered if I had fared any better. He reached inside his parka and pulled out a tobacco pouch, retrieved a cigarette that he had made earlier and lit it with the addict's practised ease. I got out of the car and waved to him. His face lit up as he recognised me. The same crooked smile, but the teeth were tobacco stained and grey.

'Hey there, Tom! Welcome back to Ireland, stranger.'

'Wow, it's good to see you, old man.'

We executed a clumsy cross between a handshake and a hug. He pinched out his roll-up and pocketed it, then lifted his bag onto the back seat and got into the car.

'You realise, don't you, that we are both old men now?' he said, giving a rueful laugh that set off a rattling cough from somewhere deep inside him. When the cough had subsided, he grinned again. 'My teeth are fucked,' he said. 'I've had a small stroke, I have emphysema and I can't walk too far, but I can still drink. Otherwise I'm in good shape.' More laughing and coughing. 'I'll be following the cousin to the grave fairly soon, but in the meantime it is good to be alive and great to see you again, mate.'

I have found that true friendships mesh again without too

much double-declutching, no matter how long the gap between meetings has been. And so it was with Tom. We clicked back into our accustomed, familiar friendship almost straight away. There was still the old air of confidence and assurance about him. But I knew that he had suffered badly from his health, and that the poise was a mask with which he dealt with the rigours of life.

We stopped for a quiet pint to get the aero-fuel fumes out of his throat. Tom sat opposite me in the comforting gloom of the pub and we chatted.

'Did I tell you that I'm playing in a band these days?' he said. 'Me and a bunch of other old farts play every Thursday night in our local. We call ourselves "The Bar Flies". I'm the drummer. We put together a CD called *The Bar Flies, Undone*. I'll send you a copy because you are probably too fucking mean to buy it, you bastard.'

The 'a' of bastard had been flattened by Staffordshire.

'Mind if I step out for a smoke?'

I ordered more pints as I waited for him to return.

'Listen, this will give you a laugh,' Tom said. 'There's something I have been meaning to tell you for ages. I've decided to get it off my chest before I die.'

'What, Tom, in the name of God?'

'Ah, you'll think I have gone mad if I tell you.'

'No I won't. What?'

He allowed a pause as he took a draw on his pint and wiped the Guinness moustache from his lip.

'You are not to be cross with me or get upset.'

'I won't, I won't. Would you get on with it in the name of Jaysus!'

'Well, you remember the night I spent at your place before we took the ferry to Holyhead to go and stay with Robert?'

'Mmm.' I lifted my pint to my lips.

'I have to tell you that I fell for your mother big time that night. God, she was a beautiful woman. I haven't lusted after anyone like that ever, before or since. I was awake for nights afterwards with all sorts of horny fantasies that would be unsuitable to tell to her only son.'

I carefully replaced my pint on the table and observed my old friend – gaunt, wrinkled, aged but still game. I laughed, and he laughed, and soon there were tears in my eyes and he had started his coughing routine again.

'Thank you, Tom, thank you. What a wonderful compliment to pay to my dear mother, who has been in heaven for twenty years now. Thanks for telling me. You poor, sad old bastard!' And we started laughing again, so that the barman began to stare over at us.

Would my mother have been horrified at the thought of such an infatuation? Or was that the prig in me denying her her conquest? Was she laughing with us in paradise?

At the end of his stay, I refused to let Tom take the airport bus; I couldn't bear the thought of my old friend, battered and wrinkled as he was, travelling to catch his plane all by himself, so the pair of us drove to the airport. I parked at the set-down area near Terminal 2.

'Remember Lolita?' he asked.

'How could I forget?'

'I remember her every time my phone vibrates in my pocket.'

'Please send my love to Louisa. I'm sure she's as beautiful as ever.'

'Of course. She's always been fond of you. Says you kept me on the rails.'

'I don't know about that. I think I always looked to your lead,' I replied.

'You were, and are, my best mate. You know that?' My friend of nearly fifty years suddenly leaned across and kissed my cheek and said, 'Cheerio, mate!'

He hauled his bag out of the back of the car and made his way into the terminal. I watched as the automatic doors shut behind him like a slow, sideways guillotine. I needed to take a few minutes before starting the car.

The First Time

The vaulted ceiling of the old converted cellar had a strange acoustic. In that crowded jolly space you could hear random conversations happening almost anywhere – at the next table, at the table by the door, at the bar. I was in the Buttery Bar in Trinity, furthering my studies as a law undergraduate, surrounded by others intent on the same goal. I was with Sammy, a friend and fellow law student. He was a robust lad from Belfast, who played rugby on the Trinity First XV and who was on an education grant from Her Majesty's government, and therefore a useful companion in the Buttery Bar.

'Have you ever noticed that lads from Ballymena can't whisper?' said Sammy, raising his voice above the echoed conversations from the other tables. 'They just lower their voices to a sort of rumble. I'm not sure what it is, but maybe it's from trying to be heard over the Lambegs.'

'Sammy, I have no idea what a Ballymena lad looks like or what a Lambeg is,' I said, surreptitiously counting my remaining few coins under the table.

'And Presbyterians always whistle when they speak. They

get special false teeth on the National Health,' said Sammy, finishing his pint. 'Do you want another?'

I felt awkward. I did not have enough for a round, and I owed Sammy.

'No thanks, Sammy. I'm OK.'

'Go way out of that, you. I can see the tongue hanging out of you with the thirst. My grant money just came through. I'm flush. What do you want?' said Sammy with a grin.

'A pint of Guinness so,' I said, somehow overcoming my qualms.

While Sammy was at the bar, I noticed two older men making their way into the Buttery. They stood out like priests in street clothes with their short haircuts, Bri-Nylon shirts and badly made suits. They were stopping at various tables, speaking to the students. Whatever they wanted seemed to cause some hilarity, and the answer seemed to be a unanimous 'no'. They arrived at our table just as Sammy returned with our pints.

'How are ye lads?' said the taller of the two, a fresh-faced bony man with red hair and big hands. 'Would you have a few moments to spare?' There was a smell of Irish stew about him.

'What for exactly?' said Sammy, looking at me and rolling his eyes.

Perhaps he was used to this in the North?

'Well, lads, we're Garda officers from Pearse Street station, and we need some lads to form an identity parade. Would you be on?'

Sammy looked at me, grinning. He winked. 'Sure, why not?' said Sammy. 'Do we have time to deal with these first?' indicating the pints.

'Take your time, lads, take your time. We need four or five others. Would ye have any pals that might come along?'

'Hold on,' said Sammy and took his pint back towards the bar, where several of his teammates were loudly congregated.

'What will we have to do?' I asked.

'Oh, don't worry about that. It will only take about fifteen minutes. You only have to stand there and let the witness have a look at you.'

'Do we get paid?'

'Ah, Lord love you, no,' said the first officer cheerfully. 'It's only a bit of civic duty.'

Sammy came back, wading through the crowding students, his pint held safely aloft.

'Paul and two others are coming. It should be a good laugh!'

Sammy's friend Paul lumbered into view. He was a huge young man, built like the side of a garage. His face looked as if it had been straightened out by an amateur panel beater. He had incipient cauliflower ears. The other two were slightly less pugilistic in appearance. It was hard to tell if they were drunk.

'How's about ye, lads?' said Paul to the policemen. 'Are ye looking for a villain? I'm your man so.' His Northern Ireland accent made the wit sharper.

The five of us made our way out of the Buttery as the other students stared, wondering if we had been arrested for something. I held myself tall, feeling like a Darnley doing a far better thing.

In the Garda station, the line-up was assembled in a biggish room with no furniture. To my disappointment, there seemed to be no one-way mirror. Three other young men were already there, and I wondered if they were the suspects. This question was quickly answered when another door opened and two Gardaí escorted a little wizened lad into the room. He was a head shorter than me, thin and wiry, with a tousle of dirty mouse-coloured hair on top of a pale face. He had a scrawny shadow of a moustache. Holding a cigarette in one of his handcuffed hands, he brought both hands and their bracelets to his mouth when taking a drag in a practised movement. His grubby clothes looked as if they had been slept in. He made no eye contact with any of the others in the line-up as he was placed between me and Paul. He dropped his cigarette butt and stood on it. One of the escorting Gardaí removed the handcuffs. I could feel the boy shaking beside me, although his face gave away nothing. This was certainly not his first time.

A female officer brought the witness into the room. She was an elderly lady in her best coat, clutching a rather battered handbag. She looked as if she had just come from Mass and was disorientated and frightened by the strange surroundings and all the young men.

'Now, ma'am,' said the female officer. 'Do you recognise the man you saw in the post office among these men here?'

The lady looked blank. Her hands were shaking in sympathy with my neighbour. The lady was walked up and down the row.

'Take your time now, ma'am. Take a good look at the men in the line-up. If you see the man that you saw in the post office, just point him out to me.'

Up and down again. The lad beside me was now shaking

like an outboard motor, perspiration trickling down from under his hairline. On the fourth pass, the old lady stopped in front of Paul, peered at him for some time, then tentatively reached out her hand to point at him. Paul, who, to his credit, had maintained a stoic straight face throughout, burst into a huge grin that unveiled his missing front teeth – casualties of an off-the-ball incident in the previous years' colours match against UCD – thus completing the look of a text-book villain, a pirate, a post-office raider.

The little lad beside me burst out laughing, all his tension releasing into a huge guffaw. This immediately infected all the other volunteers, and the grins of the Garda officers soon broke into laughter as well, while the poor old lady stood there perplexed and slightly offended.

Paul is now a retired neurosurgeon. Sammy is the chief executive officer of a multinational corporation and living in New York. As far as I know, the suspect is still at large.

Batteries Included

The man who sold me the car was later extradited to America to stand trial for the murder of his wife. He was very charming and gave me a present of a rather beautiful piece of titanium steel, which he told me was part of an artificial hip. For all I know, it might have belonged to his late wife, and sometimes I wonder if it was her ghost that had infected the little car with such an unpleasantly unreliable character. I still have the titanium and use it to sharpen my kitchen knives. I think about the murdered woman every time I use it.

The car was a second-hand Austin Mini, with a gearstick so long that changing gear tended to be something of a lucky dip. The switch for the windscreen wipers was set tantalisingly beyond reach on the dashboard, so the driver had to duck down out of sight of the road in order to turn them on. My first glimpse of the truly ugly nature of the car was about three months after I had bought it. I was scooting along the Stillorgan Road on my way home from the pub one night; there had been torrential rain that evening, and the roadway outside St John of God's Mental Hospital was flooded. I drove undaunted, without checking my speed, into the small lake that shimmered in the orange glow of the street lights. The car's entry caused a wave like the parting of the Red Sea, or an old-fashioned lifeboat launch, which I found rather pleasing in a dashing sort of way. I was sure that I would emerge on the far side, dripping but triumphant. The car, however, had other ideas. An imbecile piece of engineering design had placed the Mini's distributor cap directly behind the radiator grille, so that any splash of water was likely to drown the car's electrics and cause the car to stop. And sure enough, my car stopped in the middle of the flood, up to its axles in nasty brown water. I knew that if I waited long enough, the residual heat from the engine would dry the distributor, so my first plan was to sit tight. I lit a cigarette, a nonchalant elbow cocked out the window. At that moment an enormous articulated truck, travelling in the other direction, swept by me through the puddle and sent a sheet of floodwater through my open window, soaking me and my cigarette. It was plainly not safe to sit tight, so I took off my shoes and socks, put them on the passenger seat, rolled up my trousers, got out of the car and pushed it to the side of the road. The car spent the night beside the mental hospital. By the time I had made my way home, I was beginning to wonder whether I might have been better seeking sanctuary in the hospital myself.

Around this time, I was walking out with an especially charming young lady, for whom I had developed a strong romantic attraction. Each November, my employer organised a staff dinner dance in Jury's Hotel. A number of my workmates were going with their wives and girlfriends, and I decided to invite my own lovely girlfriend. It was a black-tie event, so my War-on-Want dinner suit got taken from its nest of mothballs and brushed down. My beloved looked utterly beautiful in her long silk gown, and she caused quite a stir among my colleagues. The evening went well, and it was after one o'clock in the morning when we strolled arm in arm to the car park. But the perfidious car decided to sulk, and it wouldn't start.

'We'll have to push-start it,' I said.

'What?'

'The battery must be low, that's all. We'll have to push-start it.'

She stared at me and said, 'What's all this "we", paleface?'

'Well, I've no money for a taxi, and I can't push her by myself because we're on a bit of an uphill slope here ...'

'You aren't joking, are you?'

'Afraid not,' I said as I got out of the car and took off my dinner jacket. With a few carefully chosen, if very vulgar, words of complaint, she got out of the car and helped me jump-start the horrid little machine in her long, glamorous dress and strappy gold sandals. I think it may have been at that moment that I realised I was in love. Although I complain about the car's vile behaviour, it may actually have been responsible for my decision to ask my wife to marry me.

Once, but only once, did that car show any vestige of loyalty. I had parked it for the night in the driveway of my house, and when I arose the following morning, I found the driveway empty. The car was gone. I don't know why I felt compelled to go to the gate and look up and down the road for any sign of the missing vehicle, but it seemed to be the natural, if futile, thing to do. And there, against all odds and to my complete astonishment, sat the car, up against the pavement about fifty yards from my gate, in an attitude of casual indifference, not quite parked but clearly going nowhere. I approached the escaped automobile cautiously, a daft part of me fearing that it might spook and run if I startled it. The driver's door was partly open, and someone had pulled the wires out from under the ignition to hot-wire it. But the thieves had not reckoned with the perverse nature of my jalopy. True to form, the battery was as flat as a pancake, and their efforts at push-starting the machine had taken them only a few yards down the road before they had decided it was not worth the effort and given up.

It had become a tradition among my friends to sing carols on Grafton Street every Christmas Eve, in aid of the Simon Community. So, early on 24 December, I dutifully drove in to town and abandoned my little car illegally on the pavement outside St Andrew's Church at the end of Suffolk Street. It had been dark when I left home and I needed my headlights, but by the time I reached town it was daylight. I didn't notice that I had left the lights on as I slammed the door and made my way to join the gang for 'Jingle Bells' and 'Rudolf the Red-Nosed Reindeer'. We sang all day, collected a respectable amount of money for our cause and retired to the pub to lubricate our singing equipment after the day's exertions. It was about six o'clock when I decided to head for home. By a miracle I had not received a parking ticket. By another miracle, my girlfriend had taken a lift with one of her cousins. I hopped into the car, tried to start it and was greeted by silence. Not a murmur from the starter motor. Not a flicker. The battery was as flat as our singing had been. The traffic on Suffolk Street was jammed solid with last-minute shoppers trying to bring their purchases home. There was no hope of repeating the push-start routine because there simply wasn't space. I sat on the front wing of the car, tired, a little drunk and despairing. A chap in a rather smart Triumph Vitesse was stuck in the tangled mess of traffic just in front of me. His window was open.

'Happy Christmas,' I offered, in ironic reference to the horror of the traffic.

'Same to you, mate,' he said with a rueful grin.

A thought fluttered into my head. 'You wouldn't happen to have a set of jump leads, would you?' This was a complete shot in the dark: a Hail Mary. To my intense surprise, his face lit up.

'As a matter of fact, I do. I'm only after buyin' them yesterday and I've been dyin' for a chance to use them. Are you in trouble?'

It took a little while and some patient manoeuvring, but eventually we managed to get the two cars into mating position and the red-and-black jump leads attached by their brand-new shiny alligator clips to the respective battery poles. He started his car, and with a quick prayer to St Nicholas, I turned the key in my ignition. Success! My engine fired. We disengaged the clips and coiled the leads back into their clear plastic bag, which he stowed again in his boot.

'I can't thank you enough,' I said, barely holding back the tears of slightly tipsy gratitude.

'Not at all, mate. You're after makin' my day, so you are. Brilliant!'

And as he drove out of sight, I heard him shout out his window a cheery 'Happy Christmas', which I reciprocated hoarsely as I slid into the festive traffic in my faithless, heartless Mini.

A Dog at Christmas

I was greeted by my sister's dog with that manic hysteria that is special to cocker spaniels. The good little animal made all sorts of grunting and squealing noises to signal her pleasure to see me, and her stumpy tail wagged so hard it seemed as if her hindquarters might part company with the rest of her. Having reassured the creature that I loved her, I rang the bell and my sister came to the door, explaining that the dog was not to be allowed into the house because she had designs on the turkey.

Once inside, I greeted my sister and my parents. I found visits home at once pleasurable and stultifying, like snuggling down under the covers on a cold night only to find that you were suffocating. I was independent at this time, working as a newly qualified lawyer and making a moderate living. My sister, also visiting, was also independent. She had left home much earlier than I and, strangely, we found that we had become closer to each other since we started to make our own way in life.

My mother found Christmas very hard going. She did all the shopping, all the cooking, and most of the washing-up and tidying. But her Christmas would not be the same without these penitential rites, and she clung to them obstinately. My father considered all these matters to be women's work and contented himself with setting and lighting the fire in the drawing room, smoking and drinking endless cups of very strong tea. By the time I had arrived, my mother was in a tense fury, headed towards one of her famous 'early-Christian martyrdoms', from which there was rarely any reprieve.

I heard my sister saying to her, 'Calm down, Mum. We're here. We'll take over, the boy and me.' We had no names in our house: my sister was 'the girl' and I was 'the boy'.

'It's just that there's so much left to do. The bird is in the oven, but I forgot to weigh it; the potatoes haven't been peeled, and the sprouts need to be trimmed and cleaned. I can't find the large gravy boat and most of the good plates seem to be cracked. Your father is in there drinking tea as if nothing was happening. But I suppose it's just me fussing as usual. Silly me, spoiling Christmas for everyone as usual. Never mind, I'll just give Peter and Janet's party a miss, that's all.'

It was the family tradition for us to go to the Christmas morning drinks party hosted by my mother's eldest brother, Peter, and his wife Janet. My mother never missed this party because it gave her a vital transfusion of her own kin before the invasion of my father's family for Christmas dinner. Refusing to give in to my mother's offer of self-martyrdom, my sister and I, while dispatching a restorative glass of Champagne, checked the roasting bird, peeled the potatoes and trimmed the sprouts. We then hauled our mother off to Uncle Peter's. My father, who was sketchily tolerant of my mother's family, stayed at home.

My father was an alcoholic but had given up the drink about six years previously and remained bravely and stoically on the wagon for the rest of his life. He was not priggish or resentful about others' drinking habits, but I think that this extraordinary self-discipline had taken some spark out of him. He certainly lacked the easy enthusiasm of my mother and her family. There were any number of good reasons why my mother excused him from Uncle Peter's annual shindig.

The party was in full riot when we arrived. Auntie Janet bravely stoked the hostess trolley with cocktail sausages and mushroom vol-au-vents, while her three sons sloshed out the drink. Uncle Peter, glass in hand, held court in his drawing room, smoking a cigar and talking for Ireland. Uncle Peter's younger brother, Bernard, and his eight children were already there. Other friends and some of Auntie Janet's relations made up the numbers. We threw ourselves into the melee of cousins. After a while, my sister noticed the time and signalled me to lasso our mother to bring her home. Easier said than done when the mother got in among her own with a gin and tonic in her hand. As was the tradition, the farewells took at least half an hour in the hall, my mother ignoring our chivvying and occasionally escaping into one of the other rooms to say goodbye to someone she had overlooked in the first round. Finally, with our mother in good fettle, and the martyrdom at least postponed, we set off for home. We found my father asleep by the fire, with my sister's dog snoring at his feet. The dog was banished to the garden again.

My sister checked the bird while I spread the fine white damask cloth and set out the places. The best bone-handled knives, the silver forks and spoons, the candelabra and the cut glass were put in place. My sister agreed that it all looked as it should, and we toasted the Christmas table with another glass of Champagne.

Then the doorbell rang. My father answered it. It was, again per tradition, my Uncle Bernard and his eight children, fresh from Uncle Peter's party, calling in for a final glass of something before driving home to Rathgar. A small stampede of my cousins came leaping and bounding up the steps of the house ready to give my father a Christmas greeting on both cheeks. He, not being a tactile man, recoiled in horror, exclaiming, 'No kissing, please! No kissing!' Nothing daunted, they fell to hugging him in a manner that seemed to disturb his dignity.

My mother joined us in the drawing room, and a glass of whiskey was put into Uncle Bernard's hand. He took up position by the mantelpiece with his back to the fire and, encouraged by his children, he gave us 'The Pride of Petravore', followed by 'The School at Killaloe'. We all joined in on: 'We learnt to sing it easy, we learnt the Marsellaisy; Toulon is on the Continent, we learnt at Killaloe.' When Uncle Bernard was into his third whiskey and was encouraging my mother to sing 'The Man Who Broke the Bank at Monte Carlo', the phone rang. I answered it, and there followed the same conversation that I had had for the previous ten Christmases.

'Hello. This is your aunt Mina. Is Bernard there?'

'Yes, Aunt Mina.'

'Well tell him that he should have been home an hour ago. The dinner will be ruined. Goodbye!'

Aunt Mina was daunting when under full sail. The

farewells started again, morsels of songs were pulled out of the air, kisses were bestowed on anyone who was prepared to receive them and Uncle Bernard and his eight offspring crammed themselves back into his car and set off for Rathgar at a speed that was intended to make up for the lost hour.

Peace descended on the house, and my sister and I encouraged our mother to sit for a while by the fire in the drawing room while we attended to the final touches of the preparations. I set about dealing with the smoked salmon. It had been bought as a whole side, unsliced, so the challenge was to carve wafer-thin slices and platter them up for each guest. The only knife I could find was rather blunt, so I had to hack at the poor salmon as best I could.

My father's brother Jim and his wife Aileen were vegetarian, so they were getting grapefruit as a starter. I halved the grapefruit and excavated the flesh into segments. I tasted one, and it was so sour that I felt my head shrink. My eyes watered and I lost the power of speech for some moments. I poured several spoonfuls of sugar on to ease the savage sting of the fruit and stuck a cherry on top.

My father's sister Ellen was first to arrive. She was a single lady who worked as a nurse. She was tall and elegant and spoke with a wonderful deep drawl. Like all my father's siblings, she had been educated in England before the war and had never lost her slightly English accent. All her nieces and nephews adored her because she was good fun and very kind. My father opened the door to her but forgot about the banished dog. While we were making a fuss over Aunt Ellen, getting her a drink and taking her coat, the dog ghosted into the hall without any of us noticing.

I was fetching some coal for the fire when I heard my sister's anguished squeal from the dining room. I put down the coal bucket and stuck my head round the door.

'What's up?'

Terrified our mother would hear, she whispered hoarsely, 'Someone let the fucking dog in and she's eaten all the smoked salmon.'

The dog, meanwhile, was wriggling and crawling around in abject self-disgrace in the way that only a delinquent spaniel can, pleading desperately for forgiveness for her own canine frailty, and looking so … well, hangdog that I ended up laughing.

'It's not bloody funny. What are we going to do?'

'I think there may be enough salmon left to serve up replacements,' I said. 'For God's sake don't let the mother know what's happened.'

So we opened another bottle of Champagne, and I set to with the blunt knife to carve some more salmon for the carnivores. The dog was ushered out of the front door with a very unseasonal lack of ceremony. It had started to rain.

Shortly afterwards the doorbell rang. It was my Uncle Jim and Aunt Aileen. Uncle Jim was one of the only reasons that my mother tolerated Christmas. He was a charming, witty man, who had a captivating way and an extraordinary charisma. My father and he were very close, and they always sparkled in each other's company. For my father, and I must say for me too, Christmas had now formally started.

My Aunt Aileen was another matter. She had been raised in London and schooled in England. She spoke with the accent of the English upper classes, and she freely and frankly admitted that she thought that Irish people were all bogmen and gombeens. She was hard going in conversation. She lacked small talk, I suppose. She was also a rabid atheist.

'Happy Christmas, Aunt Aileen.'

'Oh, do you believe in all that?'

'Well, yes. It's the time of peace and goodwill, isn't it?'

'Oh, do you think so?' Her smile was more a showing of teeth than a sign of friendship.

'Um ... Let me take your coat ...'

In the midst of all this, Uncle Jim said that he had left some presents in his car and went back outside to get them. I ushered my prickly aunt into the drawing room and poured her a glass of dry sherry. My mother tried to encourage a tiny seed of conversation with her in-law but found the stony ground unreceptive.

'I hope you are well, Aileen. To your good health,' and she raised her glass.

'I'm not at all well, but that can't be helped. Thanks for having me.'

The total absence of any social grace was awesome. My mother remembered that she urgently needed to find the gravy-browning and excused herself. My father was deep in conversation with his sister Ellen and most of this passed him by. I heard the front door slam, and my Uncle Jim came in with a cardboard box filled with potted hyacinths.

'Bearing gifts! Bearing gifts! Same old boring things as last year I'm afraid.'

We assured him that Christmas would not be Christmas without the lovely scent of his hyacinths.

'Oh, by the way, I found a poor little dog outside in the

rain. I hope it was alright to let her in?'

I bolted from the room, crossed the hall in a stride and flung open the dining-room door in time to see the dog wolfing the last piece of replacement smoked salmon from its plate.

'Oh, sweet Jesus, Mary and Joseph!' I swore in seasonal mood. I yelled for my sister and together we surveyed the scene of the crime. The recidivist perpetrator, who, as you will remember, was out on bail, sat looking sheepish while she licked the last of the fish oil from her chops. The haunted look in her eyes indicated a plea of guilty, and without further bidding she slunk over to the corner of the room awaiting sentence. This time it was my sister who started the laughter, which was tinged with hysteria and brought us both to tears.

Not only had the dog eaten all the salmon again, but on the repeat offence she had taken care to put her front paws on the table on each side of each plate as she ate, leaving two muddy paw prints on the damask at each setting. The imperative to keep our mother in the dark was even stronger now. My sister took charge of the dog and put her in solitary confinement in my parents' car, with the window open a crack. Meanwhile, I refreshed our glasses, struck the settings from the table and stripped the damask, turning it over to hide the worst of the mud stains. I then reset the table and again attacked the remains of the side of smoked salmon, offering up a silent prayer of gratitude to my ancestral gods that my mother had over-catered in the cured-fish department. Loaves we had none, but somehow the fish stretched to allow me to scavenge enough to serve Aunt Ellen, my mother and my father. My sister and I were condemned to share the acid grapefruit with the vegetarians. We drank another glass and called everyone to the table.

The dinner was a triumph.

I cooked the dinner the following year, when my mother gratefully retired from Christmas-dinner duty.

The Slippery Slope

'Oh, God. He wants to be an actor. All that education down the drain!' my mother sobbed down the phone to my sister. 'Why can't he be a solicitor like his father and his grandfather?'

I had experienced some highs in Trinity, but the best of these was the heady buzz of theatre. I became hooked. And when I graduated with a decent law degree, I was still dazzled by the glare of the footlights and giddy from the rush of performance; I could not bring myself to turn my head toward the fusty world of parchment, precision and convoluted logic that beckoned me in the family tradition of legal practice. I decided, instead, to go on the stage.

To pay the rent, I took a job as a part-time hotel porter in a single-star hotel on the North Circular Road and flung myself at the mercy of the gods of theatre, working as an unpaid actor on the outer fringes of the alternative circuit by night. But after three years of scrape, graft and privation, I realised that I needed a better day job to support my continuing thespian addiction.

The advertisement in the jobs-vacant section of the

Evening Press that I picked up off the floor in the pub caught my attention: 'Major invoice discounting firm seeks young, dynamic applicants interested in a career in financial services.' It gave a phone number. There was no specification for qualifications or prior experience. I seemed to myself to be an ideal candidate. I had no idea what invoice discounting was, but it had to be a better bet than the horse I was on. I asked my supervisor at the hotel what invoice discounting was.

'Something to do with supermarket price wars, I think.'

'But I think it's something in financial services.'

'If you know so much, why ask me? Get on with your work.'

The director of the play that I was rehearsing was sure to know, so I asked him.

'Invoice discounting? Something to do with voice and counting. Maybe it's to record that voice you hear in the lift, you know, "First floor, ladies' underwear and haberdashery. Going up." I guess someone has to do it. Now, could you try that speech again, but with more existential angst? OK?'

I phoned the number and, to my total amazement, was given an interview. But it did not seem to go well. It took place in an office in Foster Place. There were three interviewers: two managers from the department where I would be working – supposing that a miracle happened – and a nice, pretty lady from the HR department.

'And tell me, why have you applied for this job?'

'I'm not happy in my present job, and I need to move on.'

'You understand that that would not normally be a good reason for us to employ you? What do you know about our business?'

'Oh, you are a major player and need explosive

employees.' This clever translation of their advertisement was greeted with blank stares. I ploughed further into the mire. 'Dynamic has the same Greek root as dynamite, you know. Boom Boom!' I chanced, immediately regretting my gauche little effort at humour. There was a short, astonished pause. Plainly none of them watched Basil Brush.

'Yes … Anything else?'

'You probably pay much better than I am paid at present.'

'Aha, aha. Anything else?'

'Well …'

There followed a silence, during which I listened to the cooings and flappings of two pigeons who were hard at it in the plane tree outside the window. There was a glass of water on the table, which I grabbed like a suicidal drowning man and gulped it down. The HR lady was scrutinising my three-quarter-page CV, from which I had carefully excised all reference to my law degree for fear that it might contaminate my efforts at finding a less stultifying career.

'I see that you have been working in the hospitality industry for the past year. How have you found that?'

'Well, working as a part-time hall porter isn't very stimulating. I was looking for more of a challenge.'

'And what drew you to us?'

She was clearly giving me a lifeline, so I decided to make the most of it. 'I've always thought of invoice discounting as an ideal career. It's been one of my interests since before I left school.'

'And where do you see yourself in five years' time?'

'Well I hope to be working with you guys.' I paused, waiting for laughter but none came. 'Perhaps as a manager by then,' I added hurriedly. This did better by way of audience reaction. The pretty lady from HR smiled at me.

'You say in your CV that you are working as an actor. Where are you performing?'

'Well I'm not actually in a show at present.'

'And where have you performed. In the Abbey? The Gate? With RTÉ?'

'Um ... I'm more involved in alternative theatre at the moment, so you may not have heard of the venues.'

'But you said that you weren't in a show?'

'Well, yeah, but if I was, you know? Places like upstairs above Foley's pub in Dolphin's Barn, or the Micro Theatre in the corner of the Dandelion Market. You know. Alternative.'

'I see.'

There was another pause. I couldn't hear the pigeons anymore; they seemed to have concluded their feathered fornication. Maybe they were having a cigarette.

'Thank you very much for your application and for taking the time to talk to us. Goodbye.'

Ten days later, in my Dartry bedsit, on the battle-scarred Formica kitchen table with the cigarette burns and the chipped edge where some tulip had tried to open a bottle of beer, I looked at the envelope that had been delivered in the post the day before. It was clearly addressed to me, but nobody in the building had thought to let me know it had arrived. I had found it by chance in a pile of junk mail and orphan bills in the communal hallway. I wiped most of the butter from my knife and slit the envelope. To my total astonishment the letter said that I had been called for a second interview by the invoice discounters. It was scheduled for 8.30 a.m. the following Monday at the address in Foster Place.

I had my suit dry-cleaned and bought a new shirt. My shoes were so shiny that I could see up my nose in the toecaps. I had asked a bank teller what invoice discounting was, and she told me that it was to do with debt collection. The following Monday morning, armed with this misinformation and dressed as smartly as an accused felon in court, I felt ready for round two of the job-interview process as I left the bedsit in good time. I hopped into my decrepit Mini and immediately sensed tragedy. I stuck the key in the ignition, twisted it and got only a sinister sort of click that informed me from bitter prior experience that the battery was flat. I realised then that the interior light had not shone with its usual cheerful yellow when I had opened the door. It had shown, instead, a sullen shade of amber that betokened exhaustion, and when I reopened the door to get out to release some tension, it finally gave up the ghost altogether.

I looked around for anyone who might help to push-start the car, but at 7.30 in the morning, few enough citizens were stirring, and none were close enough to hail. I released the handbrake, checked that the ignition was in the 'on' position and that the choke was fully pulled out. With one hand on the steering wheel and the other holding the edge of the open driver's door, I started the painful process of pushing the traitor car until I had wound it up to a sufficient speed before jumping in, jamming the gear-lever into second and popping the clutch. It took three goes, but finally the engine kicked and I roared off in a cloud of exhaust fumes and a welter of sweat.

The traffic on the Rathmines Road had congealed to the

consistency of cold porridge by the time I joined the happy conga of commuters. I was afraid to look at my watch. I inched my way to Drury Street, where I found parking in an underground bunker manned by members of one of Dublin's most notorious crime gangs. Then I took off like Eamonn Coghlan. I dodged slow-moving pedestrians with the agility of Gareth Edwards sidestepping the English defence, bounced off the bonnet of a Ford Cortina, causing both me and the driver to swear violently, launched myself onto Wicklow Street and turned on the afterburners. I noted a personal best when I hit the corner of Weirs Jewellers and glanced up at the elegant clock to check on the time. Three minutes to go. Then disaster struck.

Some midnight celebrant had lost the run of themselves and had copiously performed the Heineken manoeuvre on the pavement on the corner of Wicklow and Grafton, leaving a minor lake of puke right in my path. I frantically applied my personal brakes and tried again to sidestep, but it was too late. My right foot went from under me as I tried to take the corner. My hands went out in a desperate bid to right myself, or at least to cushion my fall, while my feet frantically fought for traction, but all was in vain. I landed heavily on my left hip and measured my length in that puddle of puke, sliding like a crashed motorcycle racer sideways into the mainstream of pedestrian traffic on Grafton Street.

The walking public stepped over me in the practised way of Dubliners. To them I was just another body on the ground. Nobody stopped to help me. Somewhere in the trajectory of my skid I had accidentally swept up some street litter, including a partly empty chip bag, what might have been a burst balloon and a paper cup. A kindly passer-by dropped two pence into the cup.

I lay on the bricks of Grafton Street for a moment as I collected my thoughts. My hip hurt like hell, and I wondered if I had broken it. I had not hit my head, but I felt dizzy and sick. Perhaps that was because of the smell coming from the pavement. Eventually I managed to stand, and it was then that I realised the true awfulness of my situation. Not only did I look like a survivor of a stag-night debauch, I smelt like the floor of the mailboat after a rough crossing. The vile undertone of poorly digested beer made me gag. My freshly-cleaned suit was now covered from shoulder to ankle in someone else's vomit. I had managed to get it on my hands, my shoes, my new shirt and even on my socks. In the heat of the moment I forgot myself and brought my hands to my head in horror and succeeded in spreading a nice smattering of the stuff into my hair.

I needed to phone to explain to my prospective employer that I could not make it to the interview. To have turned up like this was out of the question. There was no possibility I could clean myself sufficiently to be even halfway presentable. I needed to postpone the interview until the following day. There were public payphones at the bottom of Grafton Street. I fumbled in my trouser pocket in search of coins, but I already knew I had nothing. I was right – my pockets were empty.

Despair overtook me. 'Ah, for fuck's sake,' I muttered and hunkered down to the pavement. There was a movement in my peripheral vision, and I looked up to see that my paper cup had again been donated to by a charitable passer-by. I brightened when I realised that I had now collected just enough to make that phone call.

'Thanks, mate!' I called after my benefactor. She turned to acknowledge me for just long enough for both of us to register. She was the pretty lady from the HR department.

This Is Hell

The heatwave was all well and good, but the Liffey stank like an open sewer, reaching peak levels of stink at low tide. It was the summer of 1976, the hottest summer for forty years we were told. The shudderingly rank stench had caused such a level of complaint that Dublin Corporation decided it might be a good thing to dredge it, to remove some of the noxious ooze that bubbled and belched along the river's course between the quay walls.

I had started a job as a junior conveyancing solicitor with a firm on the quays called Leetch & Co. The principal, Mr Quentin Leetch, was a bloodless man who considered each word before speaking it, like a wine taster sampling a poor vintage before spitting into a bucket. He wore rimless glasses that he kept highly polished. This gave an unnatural sparkle to his eyes, which themselves were as cold as death. Leetch's office was on the first floor overlooking the Liffey and the dredging work that was in progress.

On my first day, Leetch summoned me to his office, and I sat in an uncomfortable chair facing the river as he spelled out the rules and regulations of the firm. He read from a sort of script, delivering a list of austerely bleak workplace requirements that would have chilled the heart of a hermit.

'You are required to wear a suit and tie at all times. Personal phone calls should not be made or received. You are required to behave with decorum and propriety both during and outside office hours.'

I watched as, below me, two bright yellow bulldozers trundled on their caterpillar tracks across the vile gloop of the low-tide riverbed.

'Idle chatter, laughter, inappropriate levity or boisterous behaviour will not be tolerated. This is a place of work, not a music hall. Liaisons of any sort with the female staff are not acceptable. The hours of work are nine-to-five, Monday to Friday, but Leetch & Co. expects work to be completed in a timely manner, and this may from time to time require you to work outside normal hours.'

The bulldozers were now gathering up the unspeakable goo with its constituent bedsteads, supermarket trolleys, stolen bicycles and other treasures. Each effort brought with it a roar of diesel engines and a plume of fumes from the vertical exhaust pipes of the yellow monsters.

'You will not be paid overtime. Your lunch break is from one o'clock to two o'clock. Sick leave is only permitted on a doctor's certificate. The files and documents are kept in a central system in the basement. Anything you need should be requisitioned in writing from Mr Conleth O'Gorman, our indoor clerk, and returned again in the evening before you leave the office.'

An enormous earth-mover truck with multiple outsize tyres had appeared, and the bulldozers started to load their spoils into its vast container.

'Some of the older members of staff address me, by tradition, as Mr Quentin. You may address me as Mr Leetch. Do you have any questions?' There was a pause as he regarded me coldly.

The truck had moved out of sight with its noxious load, and the bulldozers were continuing with the dredging work. I must shaken my head.

'Very good, that will be all. Conleth will provide you with your list of cases and the files relating thereto. Good morning.'

I don't think that Leetch was aware of my theatrical endeavours. Each night and twice on matinees, bathed in sweat, I sold my soul to the Devil. The production of Marlowe's *The Tragical History of the Life and Death of Doctor Faustus* had received good reviews, and I sweltered each evening in the title role, wearing monk's robes borrowed from the Capuchins. The company of players was made up of part-time actors and students. We were performing in the tiny theatre in the corner of the front square of Trinity, which we had hired for the summer. Despite the heat, our production drew good audiences.

My Mephistopheles was a kindly fellow, given to bad puns and good friendship. Punctually, every night, my gentle devil would come to collect my soul and take it off to hell. This actor was such a genial person that I found his performance as the agent of Satan rather disturbing.

My day job was to do the legal work for clients who were buying or selling houses. I was not especially good at this work and derived very little satisfaction from it. My cases were allocated to me by the clerk, Conleth O'Gorman, an unhealthy-looking wizened man whose clothes always seemed too big for him and hung about him as if he had recently lost a lot of weight. Each morning I had to fill in a chit with a list of the files I needed that day, descend the precipitous stairway to Conleth's basement lair and hand it to him. For unexplained reasons he was always too busy to fetch me the files straight away. Consequently, I would have to climb back up the ladder-like stairs empty-handed and wait in my office for the phone to ring and for Conleth's sepulchral, nasal voice to announce that the files were ready for collection. Then back to the cellar I would go to endure a further delay while Conleth finished a phone conversation with his mother or completed some unnecessary bit of clerking before he could attend to me.

He had black hair, cropped short at the back and sides and slicked on top with some sort of oil. His face was crooked, and his jaw was shiny-blue. He would eventually deliver the required files across the table in his dungeon with an affected obsequiousness, the memory of which still chills my blood.

I had been working in the firm less than a week and had descended into Conleth's nether kingdom one morning, when he offered me one of his snarling smiles.

'I wondered if you might like to have lunch with me today?' he asked.

I felt as if I had been propositioned for something indecent but was smart enough to know that refusal would cause irredeemable offence, so I agreed.

'What a nice idea, Conleth. One o'clock, then?' I said with fluorescent brightness. I was nervous that my face might have disclosed my instinctive distaste at the suggestion, but perhaps I was better at the acting than I gave myself credit for.

'I usually take my sandwiches to the Workingmen's Club just down the quays. Would that suit you? There are chessboards available if you would like a game.'

I didn't have any sandwiches and would have to buy some before lunch, but I knew that objections or difficulties would be misunderstood. 'That would be lovely. I'll meet you in the hall at one.'

I slipped out later and bought myself a slightly stale ham sandwich in a dingy pub in Essex Street. I duly presented myself in the hall at one o'clock, and Conleth appeared from his burrow shortly after. We set off together for the Workingmen's Club. As we walked, Conleth asked me what sort of music I liked.

'I'm quite into prog rock at the moment. You know, ELP, the Floyd. Yes, that sort of thing.'

'I've never heard of that. I like the music of Barbra Streisand. Do you?'

The question was asked in the manner of a challenge. I knew better than to express my dislike for Ms Streisand's style.

'Oh, lovely,' was the best I could offer.

'I think she's wonderful. She is so accomplished as a singer and as an actress. It's such a pity that she's Jewish.'

'Surely that's not a reason for not admiring her music?' I blurted. 'I think you can admire a person's music without reference to their religion. Many of the most talented musicians are Jewish.'

'I'm a committed Christian,' said Conleth, 'and my

pastor in the Pentecostal prayer group I attend teaches us that the Jewish people are doomed to hell because they have rejected the true way of Christ. I don't like the idea of Barbra Streisand going to hell.' Conleth swivelled his eyes towards me to examine my reaction to this.

'Oh, I'm sure she won't go to hell,' I said.

By this time we had reached the Workingmen's Club. Conleth pressed the bell and the catch on the door was released. There were very few people in the club common room. My host led the way to a table by the window, which had a chessboard on it. He collected the chessmen from a shelf and started to set them up. Then he opened his satchel and took out a thermos flask and a greaseproof-paper parcel tied with a piece of brown string. He occupied the next moments with unwrapping his foul-smelling egg sandwich and carefully stowing the string in his jacket pocket. Then, still in silence, he unscrewed the cup from his flask, twisted the top and poured himself a cup of milky tea.

'Would you like some?' he offered with a strange gallantry.

'No thanks, I'm fine,' I said. For some reason I was beginning to feel queasy. There was an intimacy to this lunchtime meeting that I found creepy and abhorrent, but I could not betray these emotions to Conleth without seeming snobbish and unfriendly. I busied myself liberating my own ham sandwich from its brown paper bag. The bread had acquired a crispness that suggested it might have lain unattended on the pub shelf for some days before I had bought it.

'Pick a hand.'

'What?'

'Go on, pick a hand,' said Conleth, holding his two bony fists out in front of him. His skin was pale, as if it had never seen the sun, and his veins showed blue beneath the black hair that sprouted liberally from the back of his hands. I chose his left, which he then opened to reveal a white pawn. He swivelled the board round so that the white pieces were on my side of the table.

'I'm not really a chess player,' I said, as I made my first move.

Throughout the game, while Conleth deployed the forces of black with skill and precision, he kept up a monologue about the career of Ms Streisand on stage, screen and record. All that was required of me was to manoeuvre my white pieces so that they could be taken in battle, in accordance with my opponent's brilliant plan, and utter 'Is that so?' at intervals as another chapter in Ms Streisand's glittering career was described in loving detail. Twenty minutes later and feeling more relief than humiliation, my forces were decimated and my king was cornered and mated.

'Thank you for the game,' said Conleth. 'I really enjoyed that. We should do it again soon.'

'Yes,' I said weakly, 'that would be nice.'

But I made excuses when he invited me to lunch again. This rejection did not go down well, and Conleth exacted his revenge in small, spiteful nastinesses, like a disappointed lover. He would hide in his bunker when I needed a file or pretend that he couldn't find a file that he knew I needed urgently.

Having become exasperated with the nonsense bureaucracy of file retrieval and the petty humiliations inflicted on me by Conleth, I took to keeping some current files in my desk drawer. I had been working like this for two or three days when I received a summons from my employer to see him in his office.

'I couldn't help but notice,' said Leetch, 'while in your office yesterday, that you are keeping files in the drawer of your desk overnight instead of returning them to the central filing as required. Why is this?' He had a disconcerting habit of rolling his eyes up so that only the whites could be seen, while his eyelids fluttered like the wings of an ugly moth.

'Well they're my current cases and I found that it's easier to keep them in my desk than retrieve them every morning and return them every evening.'

'I think you will find that I am the principal of this firm. I have devised the filing system because it is the best system. I require you to follow that system, not any other system that you might find easier.' The sibilance of the word 'system' came hissing from his narrow mouth like the promise of death. Then he added, as a final flourish, 'And it has been brought to my attention that you have been late to work on four occasions in the past month. That is not acceptable.'

'But, Mr Leetch, I have never been late to work. I'm here early most mornings.'

'Would you suggest that I am lying? And would you lie to me too?' he said, the light from the north-facing windows reflecting an arctic glint from his spectacles. 'My information is quite clear. And I expect you to take better care of your time-keeping in future or I will be obliged to dismiss you. That will be all.'

I stood dumbly in front of his desk, wondering whether

further protest was wise. I decided that retreat was the best tactic and left the room. I knew, of course, that it was Conleth who had shopped me.

And while this daytime tragedy played out, by night, as Faustus, I sold my soul to Lucifer through the urbane and sensitive agency of my Mephistopheles. In the play, having summoned him to his study, Faustus asks Mephistopheles how he can appear to him if he is, as he says, in the everlasting torment of hell. Mephistopheles replies,

> Why this is hell, nor am I out of it.
>
> Think'st thou that I, who saw the face of God,
>
> And tasted the eternal joys of heaven,
>
> Am not tormented with ten thousand hells
>
> In being deprived of everlasting bliss?
>
> O Faustus, leave these frivolous demands,
>
> Which strike a terror to my fainting soul.

These lines were so apposite, coming from the lips of my gentle friend; it was typical of his unselfish nature that he would risk betrayal of his master to encourage me, Faustus, not to make the deal. This is why I found his performance so disturbing.

During rehearsals, the actor playing the part of the Pope had become romantically entangled with the actress playing Helen of Troy, and this had gradually blossomed to an affair of some passion. The Pope was a person of truncated stature, with eyes rather too pale a blue to be attractive. His fair hair tended to stand up on his head behind his domed forehead as if in shock. Helen of Troy stood a good six inches taller than him and was of substantial build, blonde also, and adequately fair of feature. As Dr Faustus, it fell to me to kiss her and have my soul sucked forth nightly, while closely observed by the Pope from the wings. This was not an unpleasant scene to play, even if the Pope's watchful gaze was a little unnerving.

> Was this the face that launched a thousand ships
>
> And burnt the topless towers of Illium?
>
> Sweet Helen, make me immortal with a kiss.
>
> Her lips suck forth my soul; see where it flies!

Unfortunately, and without interference or influence from me, Helen ditched the Pope on the morning of a sell-out Saturday performance, and he, unwisely but energetically, sought solace in a bottle of whiskey. We were unable to sober him up enough to go on stage that night. We had to announce that he had been taken ill and cancel the performance. As I was the only member of the company who owned a car, I was volunteered to drive the drunken bastard home to his flat on Sherrard Street. We had to stop more than once on the way. His parting shot was, 'I won't bore you with any crapulous excuses.' That was all very well, but he might at least have said sorry.

Distracted from my daily work by all that was happening on stage and in the troubled wings, I had taken my eye off a case and the completion was delayed. I was summoned by Leetch to explain the delay.

'I'm very sorry, Mr Leetch. I got distracted by other matters, and I forgot to raise the requisitions on title.'

'You forgot?' He pronounced the word as if he had never heard it before. The glacial panes of his glasses gave a warning flash.

'Yes, Mr Leetch. But I don't think that the vendor was ready to close. It's an executor's sale, and I don't believe that the probate has issued yet.'

'You don't think? You don't believe? The law is a matter of certainty. It is not a matter of idle conjecture.' His voice was pitched in a quiet tone but was nonetheless chilling for that. His face betrayed no emotion. He looked for the world like a dour statue on a tomb. 'What I expect from you is accuracy and attention to detail. Leetch & Co. does not pay for slovenly work. Slapstick can be delivered by clowns in Duffy's Circus.'

As my sandpapering progressed, I noticed that one of the bulldozers had trundled too far into the quagmire. For all its puffing and revving, it had got stuck; its caterpillar tracks simply churned uselessly, driving the heavy machine deeper into the mess. The driver stood and waved for help to his colleague, who set off in the other bulldozer to rescue his friend. But as he tried, with chains, to pull the stricken machine from the bog, his own tracks began to slip and skid, and soon his bulldozer was also stuck in the ghastly ooze. All the while, the tide was making its inexorable return to the riverbed, like Mephistopheles making his promised return to Faustus to claim his soul. The workers had about an hour before their machines were doomed.

Ah, Faustus,

Now hast thou but one bare hour to live,

And then thou must be damned perpetually.

Then deliverance came in the shape of a large mobile crane, the one that was used to lower the bulldozers onto the riverbed. It plucked the yellow monsters from the greedy slime and deposited them safely on the shale bank that was still above the waterline of the incoming tide. There was no such reprieve for poor Faustus.

My reverie was broken by the voice of Leetch, who had come to the end of my excoriation while I was considering the fate of the bulldozers. He raised his voice just half a decibel above his usual whisper, 'Do you understand?' The reflection on the lenses of his glasses hid his eyes completely. 'I asked, do you understand?'

'Oh yes! Oh yes indeed, Mr Leetch,' I said, as I backed out of his office.

My two worlds collided in the last week of the play's run, when I found myself beset by the gaunt, ugly figure of Conleth, lurking outside the stage door one evening after the performance.

'That was very interesting,' he said in his nasal tone, 'but very sinful. You should be very careful about summoning up the Devil, you know. The Evil One will claim your soul if you are not careful.'

'But Conleth, it's only a play. It's not real.'

'Mocking either God or the Devil is sinful and dangerous. That is what we learn at our Pentecostal Christian meetings. I'll pray for your soul.'

Without any further dialogue he sloped off across the cobbles and into the night, like a goblin of my imagination. I felt as if the dream world of my theatre life had been sullied, cross-contaminated in some disgusting way.

The run of Faustus ended just before the heatwave broke. And I handed in my notice to Leetch just before he handed my notice to me. We were not a match made in heaven, or even in hell.

A Quick Study

The phone call comes as a surprise. 'Hi, it's Bob.' His deep Californian drawl is unmistakeable. 'Listen, could you take over the part of Jasper for me? Tim has decided to drop out. We have the weekend. I know it's tight but you're a great actor and I hear that you're a quick study. Come over to my place tonight and I'll give you your script.'

Of course I say yes and pick up the script. My character is a junior lecturer in politics who can't shut up. In the first act, he believes that it is acceptable and entertaining for him to lecture his fellow guests (and, incidentally, the audience) at a dinner party, for three unbroken pages of script. In the second act, he tries to bore a young woman into bed with a further two-page monologue about the symbiotic dynamic between Marxist-Leninism and modern capitalist social structures. I have two days to learn this rubbish.

The bearded Bob, who is the director, is staying in a garden-level apartment in a large house in Killiney. He has the use of an indoor swimming pool and sauna in the grounds. It is summer and the weather is unseasonably fine. I pace the garden with the script in my hand, bashing the lines into my memory while the bees noisily gather nectar and pollinate everything in their path. By midday on day two, I announce that I am ready for a line rehearsal. Bob calls the rest of the cast for two o'clock and suggests that I relax and have a swim and a sauna in the meantime.

'But I don't have my togs or towel.'

'Togs?'

'I mean swimsuit.'

'Hey, man, be cool! You don't need a swimsuit. We always swim au naturel here. Relax! Enjoy!' He turns to go back to his flat, then calls over his shoulder, 'We have some people from the US visiting this morning, but they won't interfere with the line rehearsal.'

Annoyed and embarrassed by my own prissiness, I make my way to the pool house and push through the glass-panelled door. The air in the pool house is heavy with steam and chlorine, and the sunlight beaming through the skylight gives a tropical warmth to the space. The water of the pool reflects in wavy ripples on the ceiling. I peel off my clothes, discard them in a heap on the bench and slide into the warm water. I swim in my drowning-man's-thrashing style, up and down the pool for a while, the words of the newly acquired script swirling around in my head. I pause, breathless, at one end of the pool, muttering the lines like a deranged compulsive. I don't hear the door open, or notice anything, until I feel the motion of the water responding to the arrival of another bather. I turn and see the other swimmer ploughing towards me in a smooth and stylish freestyle. The swimmer reaches my end of the pool and executes a flawless tumble turn. It is then I realise that my new companion is female and naked. I watch her while pretending not to. She is tall, lithe and tanned, and swims like a professional. I hover in the water while I pluck up enough courage to get out, thus exposing my puny, pale body to the gaze of this stranger. She, however, pre-empts me, pulling herself from the water at the far end with a completely natural unconcern for the fact that she has no clothes on. I guessed that she was tall, but I'm not ready for the immaculately long limbs of this young amazon who is standing hardly ten yards away from me, wringing the water from her shoulder-length, densely curled brown hair.

'Hi there!' she calls to me. 'I'm Janice. A friend of Bob's. I'm attending a summer school at Trinity. He asked me over. I believe you're an actor.'

Well actually I am a solicitor and part-time actor, but it's nice to be mistaken for the real thing, so I say, 'Yeah. I'm here to learn a part in double-quick time, and I'm just taking a break.'

'I'm having a sauna. Join me.' Having issued this commanding invitation, she strides to the pine door of the sauna, droplets of water falling from her hair and body and sparkling in the sunlight. She stands by the open door, a pre-Raphaelite vision, and says, 'Come on, slowcoach. The heat's all getting out!'

It takes an enormous effort of will not to hold my hands over my genital area as I sidle to the sauna, passing by my lovely new acquaintance, and into the stifling heat of the pine-clad sweat-cupboard. Janice follows me in and shuts the door. I plonk my bare bottom onto the wooden bench with a view to minimising my nudity, but I immediately leap up yelling, 'Jaysus, that's hot!' Forgetting all efforts at modesty, I clutch my outraged scalded buttocks.

Janice bursts out laughing. 'You Irish guys are like a caricature of yourselves! Did you really say "Jaysus"?'

'Yes. Sorry!'

'Oh, not at all, I'm Jewish anyway.'

She lifts the wooden ladle from the pail by the heated stones and pours a libation onto them, causing a wave of lava-hot steam to envelope me. She then sits beside me on the bench, causing all sorts of involuntary reactions within and about my person, which my prudish stupid inhibitions fight against with every ounce of my Catholic being. I try to think of my mother but become confused because of all the other things that are happening, and I wonder if my mother would like to be remembered under these circumstances. Janice seems to be oblivious to my rising discomfort, sitting like a tanned angel beside me in the dimly lit, stifling wooden box. Have all my dreams come true or am I being tested by the Devil? Should I stand up and be counted, so to speak, or should I say a quick decade of the Rosary? It becomes increasingly clear that the Devil is winning this one, because I am beginning to stand up in a big way. Covering my rising interest with both hands and stammering with confusion, I manage to blurt out, 'Janice, I have to make a confession. I am a poor Irish lad, and I'm not used to sharing saunas with beautiful American girls. Please forgive me if my body shows interest in yours. I don't mean any offence.' And with that, I stand up, banging my head hard against the low wooden ceiling, and make my exit. My heart is pounding, sweat is trickling and regret is oozing from every pore as my maverick member swings manfully between my legs.

I decide to have another run at my lines before I join Bob and the others for lunch. I find it hard to concentrate. My hippie being tells me that I behaved like a repressed idiot, and my sensible persona tells me that I did the right thing. If I did the right thing, why do I feel this overwhelming sense of regret?

I am late to lunch, and the conversation is bubbling as I enter the kitchen of Bob's flat.

'Oh, hi there,' says Janice, bestowing on me a beatific smile.

'So, you two have already gotten acquainted?' says Bob with meaningful weight.

I feel myself blushing. Janice seems impervious to the innuendo. I say, 'Yes, we met in the pool.' She looks even more beautiful in full light, with her unruly hair caught up in a ponytail.

Bob laughs briefly and introduces the other cast members. 'This is Brian, Elizabeth, Alice and Philip,' he says. 'I guess you know some of them already.'

I shake everyone's hand. I don't know any of them except Brian, with whom I have already performed in a stage adaptation of a scene from Joyce.

'How's it going, mate?' Brian growls. His voice is deep and rasping, in a not-unpleasant way. His looks have not improved since our last meeting. He has a mane of untamed wiry red hair rising from his head like a bush fire, and his face looks more pocked and puckered than I remember.

'How have you been since the Joyce thing in Bray?' I ask.

'Oh, good enough. I've been getting bits and pieces on the radio and some voice-overs.'

He introduces me more thoroughly to the others, who are kind and welcoming. They are all full-time professionals, and I feel a little inadequate for the second time that day. As I register this emotion, Janice stands. My mother's training makes me stand too. Janice is easily six inches taller than I am.

'Well,' she says, 'you guys want to rehearse, so I'll be off.'

'Ah stick around a bit longer, Stretch,' says Bob. 'The line rehearsal won't take long.'

'No, I've got to get moving. I've a project to finish for tomorrow before I fly out.' She turns to me, smiling a really beautiful smile. 'Break a leg tonight, man! You are a gentleman. So cool!' she says and stoops to kiss me on the lips before floating out the door.

I feel anything but cool or gentlemanly. I feel like an eejit. My mind goes galloping off on a reverie of erotic might-have-beens.

Brian interrupts my daydream. 'Let's run these lines and see what happens.'

Bob seems to have relinquished command. He's bidding farewell to Janice at the front door. The rest of the cast compose themselves, and I hold my script under the table with the sort of grip that is usually attributed to drowning men.

The line rehearsal goes remarkably well, and we go our separate ways for the afternoon before gathering again in the little theatre that Bob and the company have hired for the show. I'm feeling very nervous. Alice and Elizabeth have arrived ahead of me. Alice greets me and asks if I'm OK.

They both give me a hug and tell me I'll be great, and that I'm to break a leg.

Brian and Philip come in and settle in the men's dressing room.

'See you were working up a sweat in the sauna this morning,' says Brian, sitting in front of the make-up mirror, dabbing pancake onto his craggy features.

'Fuck off, Brian, there's a good lad,' is all I can think of saying.

Undaunted by my witty drollery, he continues, 'I think you had Bob a bit worried there. She's very beautiful, if a little tall for a stumpy short-arse like you. But, you know what they say: "It's easy to climb a felled tree".'

'I'm not telling you again, Brian. Fuck the hell off!'

He raises his hands in mock surrender and changes tack, more serious now. 'Are you all set? A bit nervous? You'll be great. You're doing a grand job on the part, by the way.'

These were heaven-sent words of praise for an actor who was about to step into the barely known.

'By the way, I won't be going to the pub this week. I'm on a movie and I have very early starts. But I'd love to have a jar and a natter with you some other time,' Brian says and gives me a warm slap on the shoulder.

The opening act goes fine for me; in fact, I enjoy a shiver of *schadenfreude* as Alice makes a hash of one of her speeches, but she is able to rescue herself. It is in the second act that disaster strikes as I drone on and on in my hugely boring and impossibly long speech. My subconscious must still be toying with memories and fantasies of Janice, which may be why my concentration fails and my lines forsake me, leaving me dumb and paralysed, my mouth opening and shutting noiselessly like a salmon on grass. My mind is completely blank, devoid of cognitive function. The lights are blazing down on me like a desert sun. There seems no hope of rescue from this quicksand of silence. Then, from nowhere, Brian chimes in with a life-giving impromptu edit of the scene. His ad lib is as surprising as it is heaven-sent.

After the curtain, Bob and the whole cast give me a group hug and tell me I am great. I thank Brian for his quick thinking and generosity.

'No problem,' says Brian. 'You can buy me a pint next Wednesday in the Pembroke.'

'I'll buy you two,' I reply.

The run of the show ends that weekend. Brian does not come to the quiet end-of-show celebration, but I remember that we have a date for next Wednesday and that I owe him a debt of gratitude.

The following Wednesday evening I turn up at the Pembroke Inn and go looking for Brian. I am aware that I am one of very few men in the pub that night, but I dismiss the anomaly as being irrelevant, buy a pint and continue my search. I trawl the crowded and rather shrill pub and find myself back at the front snug, when I hear a familiar deep and rasping voice calling my name. I turn to find possibly the ugliest woman I have ever seen, leering at me with a pint in her hand. Her face is ravaged and weather-worn; her blonde hair is tied with a blue ribbon and she has far too much make-up on her eyes. She looks like a veteran from the ranks of the ladies of the night that ply their trade on the nearby square. I gape involuntarily before the penny drops. It is Brian, in full drag, grinning amiably at me with a pint in hand. He is barely recognisable in the blonde wig, full make-up, dress and high heels. No wonder I missed him on my first sweep of the pub. He does not make a good-looking female. He watches my discomfort and my struggle to maintain some semblance of poise. His grin becomes broader and he starts laughing as he puts his arm around my shoulder.

'You should see your face, man! You look as if you've caught your mother in bed with the milkman!'

I find my composure, somewhere down around my ankles, and make a better effort at greeting my friend. 'Sorry, Brian, I got a bit of a surprise.'

'The full drag? Yes, it gives most people a bit of a jolt, all right. I'm not gay, by the way, in case you're disappointed if I don't make a pass at you.'

'Let me get you a Babycham,' I say.

'Fuck off and buy me that pint you owe me. Guinness please.'

Billy's Will

On a street of decent houses, this one looked exhausted and unloved. The paintwork was peeling away, showing green under scabrous disintegrating white. The front hedge had run wild, overhanging the pavement and almost totally blocking the front path. The street lighting, on this chilly October evening, had managed, somehow, to avoid the house, so that it seemed to have pulled itself back into the shadows. No lights showed in the dark windows. The bell had been pulled from its socket, and it dangled by a single wire.

I tried the knocker and waited on the doorstep with my brand-new briefcase in my hand. I had qualified as a solicitor less than a month ago. I didn't feel like a lawyer; I felt juvenile. But my new boss had asked me to visit the client and I hadn't had the courage to say no.

I could hear voices coming from inside the house, but it appeared nobody wanted to open the door. Someone seemed to drop something heavy in the hallway and a man's voice said, 'Bugger. I've got coal all over the floor. Look what you've made me do!'

I felt that this was not the right time to knock for the second time, so I waited, afraid to go forward and afraid to go back. Eventually, having let enough time elapse to satisfy myself that nobody had heard or was prepared to respond to my first knock, I knocked again. I had meant the second knock to be just a shade louder than the first, but in my anxiety I struck the knocker timidly and without conviction. The noise seemed to me to be hesitant and limp. The door remained closed.

I heard footsteps coming towards me on the other side of the door, and a woman's voice said, 'Don't blame me because you spilled the bloody coal. Pick it up for God's sake. That solicitor'll be here any moment.'

Still nobody came to the door. After what seemed like an age, I knocked for a third time, this time with a firmness that belied my nervousness.

The man said, 'Shit! There he is. Knocking like a bloody bailiff. Maggie, give me a hand with this, it's all over the blasted hall!'

I heard shuffling and stumbling and feet retreating from the door. I was about to knock a fourth time when the door was opened by a small, spare, elderly woman. Her shabby clothes looked as if they had at one time been of good quality. She had composed her face into a smile to greet me, but she looked bothered and there was a smudge of coal dust on her cheek.

'Good evening, ma'am. I'm from Kyles Solicitors.' I gave her my name.

'Ah, good evening. I'm Maggie Phillips. Thank you for calling round to us.' We shook hands. Her grip had the knobbly reticence of arthritis. 'Please, do come in.' She stood back from the opened hall door and waved me into the house. She seemed to be unaware of her shabbiness, just as she was unaware of the coal dust on her cheek. She held herself with a certain poise and spoke with the sort of Anglo tone that my parents would have called 'educated'.

'Billy's in the drawing room, please go on in. I'll get some tea, or would you prefer a drink?'

'Oh, please don't go to any trouble for me, Mrs Phillips. I don't need tea or anything, thank you.' I made my way into the house. The hallway was narrow and dingy. The linoleum was cracked and lifting. One panel of the door to the drawing room had been broken and jammed crookedly back into place. There was a slight gaseous smell of garbage.

I entered the drawing room, repressing my rising feeling of shock at the state of dilapidation of the house. I was greeted by Billy Phillips, who was still struggling with the bucket of coal. He turned to greet me, abandoning the coal bucket in the centre of the squalid room.

'I didn't catch your name, I'm sorry. I'm Billy Phillips.' Again, a posh accent – a relic of an English public-school education. He extended his hand in greeting. It was stubby, mottled with liver spots and filthy with coal dust. Billy was a short, heavy-set man, nearly as wide as he was high. His skin had a yellowish unhealthy tinge, and he had many small growths on his face, some of them brown, some flesh-coloured. His eyes were almost hidden by folds of skin and a massive pair of ginger-and-white tangled eyebrows. I knew that he was nearly eighty, but he could have been older.

I shook my client's hand and repeated my name. I could

smell liquor and guessed that he was not sober.

'Sit down, sit down, please.' Billy waved his hand at one of the armchairs by the fireplace with its empty grate. The chair was sagging in the middle. A strap of webbing hung from below the seat, and a tear in the upholstery showed a tuft of horsehair. I sat carefully at the edge of the battered chair, trying to avoid any springs, and at the same time worried that my client might take offence at my diffidence.

Billy said, 'Well I suppose you know that I want to re-make my will to exclude my daughter from any benefit?'

'Yes, Mr Phillips.' I took out a notepad from my briefcase and sat in a rather prim position on the edge of the armchair with my briefcase on my knees and the notepad on top of the briefcase. The clock on the mantelpiece was stopped; I glanced at my watch. I carefully wrote the date and time at the top of the page along with the name of my client and the words 'Will Instructions'. Then I waited. Billy seemed to have lost interest in me. I heard the clink of bottle on glass. I was afraid to look up in case my face might betray the horror I was feeling. I heard Billy shuffling back to the fireside. Matches rattled and one was struck. A cigarette was lit. It was quite dark in the room. The only illumination came from a naked bulb standing in a shadeless standard lamp in the corner beside Billy. The wreck of a lampshade lay capsized on the floor. Billy coughed and cleared his throat but still offered no instructions. It was now quite clear that he was drunk and on his way to getting drunker.

Maggie came in and closed the door. At last I found the courage to look up from my notepad. I wondered if she should be present for my meeting with Billy. I glanced quizzically at

Billy. He took a gulp from his whiskey and said, 'Oh, don't mind her. She's getting nothing either. But she has some stuff of her own. She'll be alright.'

Maggie gave me an encouraging smile and sat in the chair on the other side of the fireplace. There didn't seem to be another chair in the room. Billy was standing, swaying slightly, by a heavy mahogany table on which stood a bottle of Jameson surrounded by dusty clutter. The table was piled with old newspapers and what looked like title deeds. There were deeds on the floor too. In the corner of the table there was an ashtray overflowing with cigarette butts.

'Those are the title deeds belonging to my ex-clients,' said Billy, waving a proprietorial arm over the strewn mess. 'I've been trying to sort them into proper bundles, but they seem to have got into a hopeless muddle!' He was smiling in a strangely triumphant way, as if this state of disorder and chaos was only to be expected. 'Did they tell you that I was a solicitor? That is until the bloody Law Society yanked my practising certificate.' He took another pull at his glass, then put it down clumsily among the parchment and cigarette ash and lifted the bottle to refill.

'I, William Bentink Phillips, being of sound mind and body,' he chanted, with heavy irony, 'declare this to be my last will and testament and hereby revoke all others. I leave my entire estate to the Royal National Lifeboat Institution. That's it. You can go home now, sonny.' He seemed to be exhausted by the effort of this, and he looked around for something to sit on. He whipped an old newspaper from the table, spread it on top of the coal bucket like a waiter with a tablecloth, then eased himself down to sit on it.

I jerked to my feet. 'Please Mr Phillips, sit here, I don't mind standing.'

At the same time Maggie said, 'Oh for Christ's sake, Billy. Bring a chair in from the dining room!'

A pause developed. Then I blurted, 'I probably don't have to remind you that the Succession Act requires you to make proper provision for your children.' I immediately felt stupid. Of course Mr Phillips would know this.

'Oh, I've provided for her alright. More than enough over the years. She's not getting another penny.' There was a snarl in Billy's voice.

'I'm afraid that Rosemary has been a disappointment to us,' said Maggie, in a tone of deepest sadness. 'She's rather gone off the rails.' There was another pause as Maggie glanced at Billy for his confirmation that she should go on. 'She was a very talented artist. She was in her final year at the National College of Art when she met the dreadful, dreadful man she's now with. She was a part-time volunteer at a homeless shelter, and he was one of the ... "guests", I think they call them. He's a hopeless drug addict. She, sort of, fell under his spell, I suppose, and got hooked on heroin herself. She says that they are married, but I'm not sure if that's true. I'm afraid she's lost to us now. The addiction has taken over her life completely. She doesn't seem to want to stop. I've no idea where they are living. The two of them turn up here sometimes, always looking for money. For drugs, of course.'

'Time for some tough love,' said Billy, standing to refill his glass then sitting again on his improvised seat. He was quite unsteady and nearly ended up on the floor.

'Will you for God's sake get a chair, Billy!'

'This's fine. Just fine. Just fine. Thing is, she is completely hooked on that bloody heroin. Hooked. And she doesn't seem to have the ... whadoyoucallit to get off it.' He turned to me in his frustrated search for the word, his right hand making little spirals in the air. 'Whadoyoucallit? The will. That's it. She lacks the will. Willpower. Time for tough love. I may have bugger all, but she's getting none of it!' He put his glass on the floor and searched his pockets for cigarettes. After he lit one, he dropped the spent match on the carpet.

A sudden hammering on the hall door made me jump. Billy slowly rose from his seat, shuffled over to the window and pulled a corner of the faded green curtain aside. 'Oh, bloody hell! It's her, and she's got that bastard Treacy with her!' He went out to the hall, coughing and muttering, and I heard the hall door being opened. 'Go away!' shouted Billy, by the door.

'Hi Daddy.' Then louder and with increased urgency and volume, 'No, no, no, don't close the door on me! Daddy, please! I just need to talk!'

'Go away. Bugger off. You are not welcome here.'

The woman's voice shouted, 'Open the door, Daddy. Let us in, Daddy!'

There was a pause, then I heard the sound of the door being pushed from one side and resisted from the other, with the knocker beating lightly with the motion.

'Please, Daddy. I need to talk to you,' pleaded the woman's voice.

Then I heard another man's voice. 'Open the fuckin' door or I'll break the fuckin' thing!'

'Get away from my house, you piece of dirt. I'll not have

the likes of you in my house.' Billy's voice was rising in anger.

'Daddy, Sean is my husband, and you have no right to speak to him like that.'

'I'll speak to that thieving, junkie shit in any way that I like in my house. You can go now, you're not wanted here. Or have I not made myself plain?'

'Daddy, I need to talk to you. I'm entitled to some answers. Neither of us are leaving until you give us both some answers.'

There were sounds of a scuffle in the hallway. Maggie was standing now, with a look of desperate resignation on her face. I felt that I should remain seated; my briefcase and notepad were still balanced on my knees. I thought that if I was able to remain absolutely still, I might become invisible.

'Are you in on this too, Mummy?' A youngish woman with a tangle of unwashed brown hair had come into the room. She had had make-up on her face at some time in the last twenty-four hours, but most of it was smudged off and her mascara had run. She wore an orange sweater, the sleeves of which were too long for her, and she constantly tugged at them to pull them up. There was a hole in the front of the sweater. She wore dirty blue jeans and runners. She was carrying a large, very grubby, white imitation leather handbag. She fumbled in it for a packet of cigarettes, took one out and lit it with a disposable lighter. Her fingernails were bitten, and her fingers were stained with nicotine. She could have been thirty or fifty.

The scuffle in the hallway resolved itself and the man that I understood to be called Treacy came into the room, with Billy, having lost the defence of his hall door, shuffling ineffectually behind him. Treacy wore a filthy denim jacket over a yellowish T-shirt with 'Mothers of Invention' printed on the front. He wore his hair in dreadlocks, and he looked badly in need of a bath. He was skeletally thin and there was a tremor in his hands. He constantly referred to Rosemary with his eyes. Now he took her lead, like an obedient ghost.

'Rosemary's right. Yous have no right to treat her like this. She's your fuckin' daughter for fuck's sake, and she's entitled to some answers.' He spoke without real menace, as if he was simply saying the words to support Rosemary. Then he noticed me and eyed me with deliberation. 'Who the fuckin' hell is this?' His voice had a high nasal whine and a sort of drawling delivery associated with long abuse of Methadone.

I had opened my mouth to speak, but Billy spoke first. 'Treacy, I have already told you that I don't want you in my house. Leave now or I'll call the guards.'

'Daddy, Sean is my husband, and he is entitled to be in this house. Call the guards if you like; they won't do anything anyway, useless fuckers.' Rosemary's well-schooled Dublin middle-class accent remained intact despite her degraded circumstances.

'Please don't use language like that,' said Maggie.

'Give us one of them will ye?' Sean nudged Rosemary, indicating her cigarette. Rosemary gave him a cigarette and the lighter. His hands were trembling so hard that he could hardly light the cigarette.

'Rosemary, your father and I have made it clear to you before that Mr Treacy is not welcome here. He has destroyed your life with his drugs and his stealing and his prison terms. He is not worthy of you, and we want you to leave him. He is common trash and he should leave the house right now.' Maggie's Anglo accent was stronger with her emotion and the stress of the situation.

'And you can go and fuck yerself, so you can, you stupid, stuck up, posh auld bitch!' Treacy mumbled. 'Rosemary is me wife and there's nothing yous can do about that. We're here for answers and we're not leaving till we get them, so we're not.' Mid-speech, his voice seemed to become disengaged from what he was saying. It seemed like he was gradually losing his train of thought. I noticed that his eyes were half-shut, as if he were on the verge of sleep. He was plainly high on something.

'You'll get no answers or anything else out of me,' said Billy from the doorway. 'You have pissed away Rosemary's inheritance and anything else we were able to give her, and now you have her on your poisonous drugs as well. Clear off, you bastard of hell!' His anger had sobered him up a bit.

Rosemary said, 'I'm entitled to know what happened to my trust money, Daddy. You are my trustee and you have to tell me. Where is it? What have you done with it? Tell me. Now!'

'I'm not having this conversation with you while that scum is in the house. I don't have to tell you anything.'

'I know that my godfather left me ten thousand pounds in his will, and you were trustee. I haven't seen a penny of that money. I'll summons you to court if I have to. What've you done with my money?' Rosemary seemed to be on the verge of tears, but I wondered if she had many tears left in her.

'Yea, you dirty, thieving auld scumbag. Where's Rosie's fuckin' money?' Sean was standing too close to Billy now.

His body was making little unhappy involuntary twitches, and the ash on his cigarette was too long. He fished in the top pocket of his denim jacket and produced a syringe. 'I'll fuckin' stick you with this. I swear to God. I'll fuckin' do it!' He held the syringe to Billy's throat.

Billy didn't flinch. 'Go ahead. I'm dying of cancer anyway. HIV or AIDS won't have time to do much to me. Just get to hell out of here and take that poor little tramp with you.'

There followed a silence so long and profound that I could hear my own breathing over the peculiar noise made by Sean's tremor and Billy's laboured wheezing. Maggie sat like a statue, silent and unmoving. I couldn't tell whether she had already known of Billy's cancer, or whether she actually cared. I felt the sweat trickle down from my armpit inside my shirt. My hair felt as if it was on end. My mind raced in useless circles as I thought desperately for something I might do, some stratagem that would allow me to get out of that house. I had forgotten all my sham dignity, all my carefully cultured poise and my idea of my status as a solicitor. Now I was just scared.

'I'll fuckin' kill ye, ye bastard.' Sean's ruined voice came sleepily from high in his throat, his buzz popping and fizzing in his brain.

'Sean, don't be stupid, baby. C'mon, honey, leave him be.' Rosemary was pulling Sean by his sleeve. He seemed to forget himself and lashed out at her with his elbow. She stepped away to avoid the blow, like a sparring partner inured to such violence, and he lost his balance. He took a step backwards, tumbling over the coal bucket, falling heavily and striking the back of his head very hard on the corner of the table. It made a strange noise as it impacted with the table; it was the sound of an axe striking a tree. His unconscious body fell clumsily to the floor by my feet.

'Oh Jesus! Sean, love, are you OK?' Rosemary was crouching by his side, his casual violence forgotten in her concern for him. She was in tears. 'Oh Jesus, God! What have you done?' It wasn't clear to me who the question was addressed to. Billy? Sean? God? She was pulling at Sean on the floor, trying to revive some life in him. 'Mummy, he's unconscious!' Her voice was that of a lost little girl. 'He's hurt himself badly! Oh, Jesus, the blood! We need an ambulance!'

'He can die where he lies, for all I care,' said Billy, stepping over Sean's legs to pour himself a drink.

I could see blood spreading and puddling around Sean's head on the threadbare ancient carpet. I lurched to my feet, stuffing the notepad into my briefcase, 'We should phone ...'

'The phone was cut off last month,' said Maggie in a hopeless voice. 'There's a phone box at the end of the street.' She was standing now, her right hand massaging her left.

Billy was leaning against the table, glass in hand. His eyes had lost focus and his breathing was laboured. He put his glass down and foostered with his cigarettes, finally separating one from the pack and lighting it as if by remote control. Rosemary was kneeling by Sean, her left knee now in the puddle of his blood. She was making small high-pitched keening noises and rocking back and forth.

'I'll go,' I said, glad of the opportunity of escape. I almost ran from the room and out the front door, leaving it ajar. I breathed in the peace of the night air. I found the phone box about a hundred yards down the street and called for an ambulance. My knees were trembling and my breathing was shallow. I took my time to return to the house, pushed open the door and waited in the hall.

Through the half-open drawing-room door, I saw Maggie, standing, watching her husband as he slumped against the table, while the pitiful vignette of her daughter and son-in-law played out on the floor at his feet.

'When did you find out about the cancer?' Maggie asked him. She struggled to keep her voice steady.

'What? Oh, at the doctor last week. Bloody quack said that I had a few months at the most. Then asked me when I thought I might be able to pay his bill! Cancer of the liver. Advanced. Ha!' He paused, drank and took a drag on his cigarette. He exhaled a stream of smoke as he looked at the ceiling. 'I've had enough anyway. No fun in carrying on the way I am.'

Maggie sat down in the chair beside the empty grate. 'Oh, Billy,' she said. She seemed to shrink. I sensed a lifetime of emotion crammed into those two words: loss, sadness, disappointment, a sense of waste and love, of a sort. Yes, love: 'Oh, Billy.'

'I stole everything I could from my clients, stole all this poor bitch's trust money.' He glanced down at the crouched, miserable figure of his daughter. 'Nothing left in the tank. Nothing left to hock. What a bloody mess. I need a drink.' He turned clumsily to reach the bottle, poured the dregs into his glass and raised it in ironic salute to his wife. 'Cheers my dear!'

Sean was dead by the time the ambulance arrived. Rosemary left in the ambulance with the remains of her husband, leaving the remains of her family in the cold unheated house, barely glancing back. The Gardaí had also arrived by this time and were taking statements with calm bureaucratic formality. I gladly made my statement, excused myself and left, gathering the tatters of my professional cloak around me. Maggie came to the door to see me off, with the automatic reaction of well-drilled manners. Her face betrayed little, but I thought I could see a final defeat in her eyes as I shook her hand and said goodnight.

A Nice How Do You Do

My father had a scunner about politicians; he felt they were all self-seeking scoundrels. At pole position in the odium stakes was Eamon de Valera. The mere mention of his name would send my father into a white fury. He considered him to be a hypocritical Holy Joe, a whited sepulchre and a bigot. He also considered him to be a traitor for rejecting the Treaty of 1922 and for causing a pointless, bitter and bloody civil war.

But Dev was dead at the time of which I am writing, and the nation was under the leadership of one Charles J. Haughey: Fianna Fáil politician, sometime Minister for Health, Minister for Justice, Minister for Finance, and now Taoiseach. And it was upon Charlie that my father had refocused his odium. My father felt that it was a matter of deep shame to the nation that its people could have allowed such a slippery trickster, such a corrupt and dishonest dealer, such scum, to be its prime minister. Charlie occupied a special niche in my father's private hall of infamy.

The invitation came in the post from the Royal National Lifeboat Institution, addressed to my father and my mother, requesting the pleasure of their company at a reception to announce the building of a new premises for the Lifeboat Station in Dun Laoghaire. At the time, my father was captain of the oldest dinghy racing fleet, and it was in this capacity that he had been invited to the event. The reception was to take place at the National Yacht Club. The NYC had among its members Dr Patrick Hillery, who was then serving as President of Ireland and who, in my father's view, was a political hack and crony of Haughey's. Hillery would undoubtedly be at the function. However, notwithstanding this impediment, my father felt that duty required him to attend, and he accepted the invitation.

Then word filtered back that the Taoiseach, the great Charles J. Haughey himself, was to attend the event in person. Haughey liked to consider himself a yachtsman. He owned a motor yacht and a small island, both of which he kept in Kerry. He liked to be photographed wearing a yachtsman's cap. He must have seen the event as a useful photo opportunity.

My father was now in a dilemma. He felt obliged to attend the reception because of his status as representative of his racing fleet, but he could not bear the thought of standing in the same room as Haughey. So he announced to my mother that they would arrive at the function early and leave before Haughey and his inevitable entourage were due to arrive. He told my mother that under no circumstances would he speak to or have any doings whatsoever with Haughey.

On the appointed day, my parents arrived at the National Yacht Club, very punctually at the given hour. My father was greeted by the club commodore, and drinks were offered. My mother asked for a gin and tonic. My father had a ginger ale and lit a cigarette.

My mother was a beautiful woman, and very gregarious. She was in her element in the yacht club, chatting to old friends and making new acquaintances. Everyone wanted to talk to her, and she was happy to talk to anyone. She mingled with the gradually growing crowd of invitees. Someone bought her another gin, which she accepted with grace. My father meanwhile was in deep conversation with the national organiser of the RNLI and the secretary of the Dun Laoghaire branch. He explained to them, as he lit another cigarette, that he would have to leave before the speeches because of another engagement, and he proffered his apologies. He then decided that it was time to leave, but he couldn't find my mother. He searched the dining room and the hallway, but there was no sign of her. Eventually he found her in the bar, in flirtatious conversation with a good-looking young man who had just bought her another drink and was clearly smitten by her looks and vivacity.

'Come on, we're off,' said my father.

'But the party's just getting going. Let's stay a bit longer.'

'No, I explained to you already, we have to leave now. Come on.'

'You'll have to excuse my husband. He's very rude.' Rather than waste it, she took a good swig of her new drink, then put it down. 'It was lovely talking to you, Roger.'

'Robert.'

'Yes of course, Roderick.' Then, to my father, she said, 'I'll have to find my coat.' She made her way down to the ladies' cloakroom in the basement of the club. My father waited in the hallway. He lit another cigarette and glanced at his watch. His eye caught my mother coming up the stairs, and at the same moment the hall door burst open and Haughey, with his coterie of minders and hangers-on, made his entrance to the club. My father stepped back, his mind still bent on escape.

Haughey was not a tall man, and he was very ugly, but he had an undeniable sort of reptilian charisma about him. He also had an eye for a handsome woman and, as he established his presence in the hall of the club, his eye fell on my mother coming up the stairs in all her glory, the best part of three gins to the good. She reached the top of the stairway and made straight for the hall door, but Haughey was between her and the door. He assumed that she was walking towards him to welcome him.

'And who is this charming lady, may I enquire?' he rasped in a sort of a purr.

My mother announced her name, holding her head high as if in defiance of the enquirer's vile charm, but failing to recognise that very famous snake in the grass. 'And whom, may I ask, have I the pleasure of addressing?' she asked guilelessly.

'I am Charles Haughey, and I have the honour to serve as Taoiseach of this country.' He didn't seem to be in the least bit fazed by my mother's failure to recognise him. He delivered his line with great gallantry. My father must have made an involuntary move towards my mother, perhaps with the instinctive desire to protect her from contamination. Haughey's hooded eyes locked onto him. 'And who is this distinguished looking gentleman here?'

'Oh, this is my husband,' said my mother, and introduced him by name. Haughey held out his hand to my father. My father was trapped. The club commodore and the national organiser of the RNLI had come out to the hallway to greet the Taoiseach, and all lines of escape had been blocked off. Impelled only by a lifetime's training in good manners, my father shook the outstretched hand of the man he considered to be the most shamefully corrupt and dishonest politician that this poor country has ever produced.

'How do you do?' was all he could think of saying. Then without further ado, he grabbed my mother by the arm and hustled her, protesting, out of the club. He drove them home in shocked silence and immediately went upstairs to have a shower.

Long Grass

My mother found the house for me. It looked wholly unprepossessing from the outside, an anonymous 1950s, three-bedroom, semi-detached house with a main road roaring past the front door. Discoloured white paint was peeling off in chunks, revealing the earlier archaeology of a previous cream-coloured paint job. Dreary green algae adorned the concrete pillars of the flat-roofed open porch. A scraggly hedge, embroidered with looping brambles and wild honeysuckle, bounded the small front garden, and in the middle of the shaggy front lawn stood a sad little monkey-puzzle tree, stunted and struggling for survival.

The front door was nicely warped, admitting, in all seasons, a gentle cooling gale. The interior was a suburban catastrophe of neglect that had seen neither love nor decorator for decades. The only furniture was a forlorn-looking black telephone, which stood dustily on the floor by the front door. It offered no communication, only silence. And yet my mother saw in this sad slum the makings of a suitable house for me. I trusted her judgement, obtained a mortgage loan and bought.

Elbow grease and paint soon gave a cosmetic lift to the house, and in due course with borrowed money, I replaced the draughty old metal windows with double glazing, glazed in the porch and installed central heating. A great deal of hard labour restored the back garden from wilderness to something more closely resembling a lawn and vegetable patch. I sowed potatoes, and when I lifted the first of the new tubers the following August, I began to feel that this place was home.

But the telephone in the hall remained silent and unresponsive. It seemed that a previous occupant, a tenant of the person from whom I had bought the house, had neglected to pay the phone bill and the line had been cut off. As soon as I took possession, I applied to the Department of Post and Telegraphs on a prescribed, triplicated form, seeking reconnection of the line, and received a non-committal acknowledgement of my application in Irish and English. But after a year there was no sign of progress. I wrote to the Department and again received a stilted acknowledgement addressed 'A Chara' and finishing 'Mise le Meas' but unsigned. Every year for five years I turned my face again to the wailing wall of the Department and begged for a connection. Each year I received the same acknowledgement letter addressing me as the sender's friend, but giving me no hope of a phone line.

In the interim much had changed in my life. I had married a wonderful girl, and she had moved in to share my semi-detached, disconnected abode.

'What are you going to do about the phone?'

This jabbed a barbed goad into my narcissistic male ego.

'What the hell can I do? I applied for a line nearly five years ago and I have been writing to the Department ever since, but nothing is happening.'

'But you're a lawyer, why don't you sue them or something?'

'Oh for God's sake, what would that achieve?'

'I thought they were bound by law to provide a service. My dad told me that there was a case.'

My piqued ego was at the limits of endurance. Her father knew more law than I did?

'Well maybe your dad would like to sue the Department then.'

'Well I'm not going to be stuck forever cut off from the rest of the world. Maybe I should go to a solicitor.'

'Oh Jesus. Just leave it, would you? I really am doing my best.'

But a goblin on my left shoulder whispered that I was taking a certain perverse pleasure in being a victim of the Department and did not want the wait for a phone line to end.

Almost exactly five years after my first application, and just before my lovely wife and I did damage to our relationship on the jagged edges of the problem, I received a letter from the Department telling me that a line would be connected within six weeks of the date of the letter. And indeed some six weeks later, a card was stuffed through the letter box to inform us that an engineer from the Department had called to the house but nobody had been home. The note said that the engineer would call again. The card gave a contact number; ironic, because we had no phone with which to call that number. Of course, this was on a Friday and outside office hours, so the following Monday I phoned the number from work and was put on hold for twenty minutes until I eventually gave up. I tried every day to contact the number, but each time I was put on hold and each time my exasperation grew until I slammed down the receiver in despair. I can never hear 'Greensleeves' now without remembering those days.

After playing this maddening game for nearly two weeks, I finally made contact and managed to pin the Department down to a specific date. I took that day off work. I was not particularly surprised when nobody from the Department turned up. My shaky grip on sanity was beginning to slip.

'Is that bloody phone ever going to be connected?'

'Don't ask me. Ask the Department.'

'You really should do something about it. Phone up and complain.'

'What do you think I have been doing for the past five years? I'm at my wits' end. Get off my back!'

My Neanderthal hunter-gatherer pride was badly wounded. The gorilla part of my brain told me that my female thought I was not functioning properly as a male, that I was incapable of providing for her, or adequately fulfilling anything else on the conjugal 'to-do' list for that matter. Clearly I was not coming up to the mark.

Then one Saturday morning, just after I had given up all hope, there was a knock on the door and a simultaneous ring on the doorbell. There stood a Posts and Telegraphs engineer, kitted out in a sort of boiler suit with a belt holding every imaginable tool to do with electrics and telephony. There was even a telephone handset in a special clip.

'Are you the man for the telephone line?'

'Yes, I am indeed.'

'We called a couple of times during the week but there was no one in.'

'That would be because we work.' The sarcasm was lost on him. I drew a deep breath and decided against shooting the dove that had arrived with the olive branch of salvation. 'Well it's great to see you. I didn't know that you worked Saturdays.'

'Yeah, well, we're not all nine-to-five men in our trade.'

I let the riposte go by. 'What do you need to go ahead?'

'Oh, it's all done, pal. You're all hooked up. Do you want to test before I go?'

And for this casual delivery I had waited for five years? The 'hooking up' required no input from me, no access to the house and seemed to be the work of less than ten minutes. I bit back all the seething anger of a righteous tax-paying citizen who had been done in the eye by a yob in a boiler suit. I took hold of the controls and steadied the personal ship. I breathed deeply and relaxed the muscles in my shoulders that had threatened to rip my shirt.

In placid compliance with his request, I picked up the handset of the ancient black plastic phone that had sat dumbly in the hall for so long and jumped with fright, or perhaps it was joy, when I heard the gentle purring of a live phone line. I signed the man's form and he left. I shouted for my wife and together we took turns picking up and replacing the receiver and hearing again and again the tone that meant connection to the outside world. My wife phoned her mother. Forty-five minutes later I tried my parents' house, but nobody picked up.

And so, for a year or two, life went on. We grew accustomed to the telephone and no longer jumped when it rang to signal an incoming call. We also grew used to the two-monthly phone bills that arrived with a punctiliousness that flew in the face of the appalling delay in delivering the service.

Then one day, a man in a van, not related in any way to the man in the boiler suit, reversed his vehicle into the telegraph pole that had, until very recently, stood so uselessly in the grass verge outside my house. Our line went down.

All the next day, I neglected my work and devoted myself solely to making hundreds of calls reporting the fault in our service. By some miracle another man in a boiler suit and many-spannered belt showed up on our doorstep within two or three days.

'Do youse have a fault?'

'We do indeed. Someone drove into the telegraph pole and our phone line was knocked out.'

'Can you confirm your phone number please, pal?' I seemed to be making lots of new friends. I gave him the number.

'We're just goin' to give you a call to make sure that the line's workin'. Do you know the phone numbers of the two houses next to you?'

I was able to give my next-door neighbour's number, but I didn't have the number of the next house along.

'I haven't got his number, but his name is Fiachra McGuckian.'

'That's an unusual name. Is he a teacher by any chance?'

'Yes, I think so. Retired now.'

'Ah, well, he'd be the bollocks that beat the head off me

every day for six years at the Christian Brothers in Glasthule.'

'Oh ... well.'

'And he can fuckin' wait for his reconnection, so he can. Happy days. I've been waitin' for this for a long time. The fuckin' long grass is sweet, as they say. So long, pal. Glad to be able to help you.'

And off he went in his Post-and-Telegraphs van. I could see him grinning to himself, and as he passed McGuckian's house he leaned across the passenger seat and raised an eloquent two fingers in salute to his old teacher.

Mending a Rib

My father went to the circus with some of his friends the day I was born. It seemed like the right thing to do, I suppose. My mother and I were safe with the nuns and nursing staff at Hatch Street, and what else would you do on a January afternoon in 1950?

As a father, he was kindly but removed. He was the opposite of tactile, preferring to avoid touching, hugging or kissing. I have flicked carefully through the box file of my memory, and I cannot think of a single occasion on which my father voluntarily touched me. On the rare occasions we came into physical contact, it felt strange and unnatural, slightly awkward and even embarrassing. His body warmth seemed alien, and he himself seemed to be tense and unwilling to the touch.

Like many boys, I spent much of my childhood and a good part of my adult life striving to achieve my father's approval. He did not mean to have this effect on me. He did not mean to be anyone's hero. I sometimes wonder if he really meant to be anyone's father. I felt that my instinctive and puppy-like clamouring for his attention and affection was regarded by him as something unseemly and undignified. It was not that he intended to be parsimonious with his praise; it was just that it never seemed to occur to him to dispense any. This saddened me and made me wonder whether he loved me or was even vaguely fond of me.

We never had what might be called a heart-to-heart conversation. I suspect that not many fathers and sons do. For my father, emotions and everything that attended them were not for show; they were for bottling up. Born into a staunch, if not particularly devout, Protestant family in south County Dublin, he had been sent to boarding school at the age of six, as was then fashionable, first to Mourne Grange School in County Down and later to Cheltenham College in England. This was thought to give boys backbone. And my father had backbone to spare. He had the strongest will and the most powerful sense of right and wrong of anyone I have ever known. And yet he was compassionate, gentle and kind, if a bit aloof as a father. It was as if he had been surprised by parenthood and was not quite sure what to do with it.

My father's diffidence as a parent was to an extent compensated by my mother's abundant and ebullient love. But the charabanc of my childhood rarely fired on all cylinders and sometimes struggled uphill with my mother pushing manfully while my father seemed to misunderstand his role.

My mother, a Catholic, had married him despite both her family's strong aversion to any faith that did not embrace Rome and his family's equal aversion to any faith that did. She was a feisty, fearless beauty, who had served in the Second World War as a nurse, and had shaken off many of the repressive shackles of between-the-wars Ireland to become a strongly independent woman. She was a hands-on mother, who could, and did, hug and kiss to beat the band (as she would say). The Pope had decreed that the children of mixed marriages must, under oath from their parents, be raised as Catholics. I was therefore sent for my early education to the Sacred Heart nuns, where, aged five, I was assured by Mother Stuart that my father was going to go to hell.

Mother Stuart was an elderly woman with a splendid moustache and tortoise-shell spectacles. Her face was permanently framed by a pleated, starched wimple that looked as if it had been made out of special white corrugated cardboard and covered with a veil of black crepe paper. It seemed to be Mother Stuart's job to teach her young charges that all Protestants, without exception, were destined for hell because of their refusal to be Catholic. Maybe that was why my father was a little remote? It would be bound to weigh on you, that sort of knowledge. My reaction to the sad news of my father's fate was one of bewilderment – a state of fuddled emotion that often visited me in my dealings with my father. However, I was certain that Mother Stuart could not be right, and I think that this sowed the seed of my own eventual split with Rome.

My father was a skilled racing helmsman and I inherited his love for sailing, if not his talent for winning races. I also inherited his racing dinghy, *Coquette*. She is built of overlapping planks of yellow pine on a framework of ribs of oak. The planks are held together and fastened to the ribs with copper rivets. My father and my mother together raced this little boat to champion success in Dublin Bay for more than twenty-five seasons.

My father's chosen position in the boat was sitting on the floor of the cockpit smoking Players' Navy Cut cigarettes, and the only part of him visible from outside the boat was his cap and a plume of tobacco smoke. Occasionally I would be drafted in to crew if for some reason my mother could not sail. Among the crew's duties was the business of lighting cigarettes for the helmsman, a service that was required no matter what the waves and the weather were doing. The fags and a Zippo lighter would be tossed in the crew's direction by way of indication that a nicotine fix was required and usually with the admonition 'Don't get them wet'. So, in hurricanes of wind, driving rain and mountainous seas, the crew was expected to take a cigarette from the packet and light it before surrendering possession to the skipper. I was usually in the throes of giving up smoking, but my efforts at cold turkey were constantly thwarted, since I would find myself obliged to light the helmsman's essential cigarette, taking a grateful gasp of smoke before passing it to my father, who would grumble that I had smoked half of it.

At the end of each season *Coquette* would be brought home to my parents' house, where she would be put in the shed to be cosseted for the winter. In early spring, work would start on getting the boat ready for the coming season: scraping, sandpapering, painting and varnishing. A combination of great age and the stresses of close-quarters competitive racing meant that from time to time repairs were needed. My father was also a very skilled woodworker, and he would effect the repairs himself where possible. I was sometimes asked to help.

One particular call for help involved replacement of a

broken rib, which was a two-man job. As always, the request for help came in the form of a summons; there was never any consideration that the time or place might be inconvenient for me. I was simply, if politely, ordered to attend on the given day at the given time. In obedience, I attended and, in accordance with the usual choreography, drank very strong tea with my father in the kitchen, conducted our usual oblique conversation about literature or events of the day while he smoked his Players, and through our system of mirrors and smoke we communicated in our way. Then we went to his workshop and started the work.

He had cut a lath of oak about the thickness of a thumb and about eight feet long. He told me he had obtained the timber from an undertaker's business that had gone under. He had soaked the lath for two days in a metal pipe full of water. To start the repair process, we had to cut out the old broken rib. This was done with much labour using a small carborundum wheel on an electric drill to mill down the tops of the old rivets. We broke up the old rib into small pieces, which we used to start a fire just outside the workshop. We emptied most of the water from the pipe and then placed the closed end over the fire and waited for the water to boil. Then we slid the waterlogged oak lath into the steamy pipe and stuffed the open end of the pipe with rags to contain the steam. The steaming continued for about forty minutes, after which we removed the lath from the steam-pipe, and while it was still hot we bent and manoeuvred it into position where the old rib had been. The hot, steamed timber was extraordinarily pliable and would readily take up any bend or twist without breaking or cracking. The procedure of manipulating the hot timber into place took a little time and coaxing, but soon the new timber looked as if it had grown there. Then it was time to start drilling and nailing. We drilled a hole through the new rib from the outside of the boat, through each old empty nail-hole, and, again from the outside, we hammered copper nails into place to grip the rib. We then allowed the rib to cool completely while we had lunch and more cigarettes and circumspect conversation.

After lunch we tapped a copper washer (or 'rove') down the length of each nail, cut off the excess nail, then one of us hammered the remaining stump from the inside to form a rivet while the other held a weight against the nail-head on the outside – the rivet clasping the new rib and planking firmly together in its metal grip. We worked without a break, completing twenty rivets, until the rib was fully installed. All this time we hardly spoke a word, and we eventually emerged from the workshop in the early evening exhilarated and exhausted, I in a trance of happiness.

My father wore himself out caring for my mother as she gradually disappeared in the miasma of Alzheimer's disease. He was taken to hospital suffering from anaemia, but the medics could not find out what was really wrong with him. He was discharged to a nursing home where my heavily pregnant wife and I visited him. He had become so weak and despondent that he lost his craving for cigarettes and, I think, the will to live. I longed to tell him that I loved him, but those words were so alien to our normal commerce that they would have sounded like a slap in the face. But I needed to say something to let him know that he was loved. Then my wonderful wife, who had been brought up unafraid of emotions and was aware of this bald spot in our dealings, took his hand and spoke up.

'You know that we love you and we want you to get better,' she said.

His tired eyes brightened with a flicker of gratitude, and he smiled and said, 'I'll do my best.'

A few days later, my first son was born, and a few days after that, my father developed pneumonia and died. At his funeral I cried more tears than I knew I had. I cried for the loss of him and for all that he meant; I cried for the love that I was never allowed to show him, and I cried for him and whatever it was that inhibited his flow of emotion. I cried in a way that he would most certainly not have approved of, but I didn't care.

I have helmed *Coquette* ever since, but with small success other than the pure enjoyment of competitive sailing. Sometimes one of my sons will crew for me if my regular crew is unavailable. Each September I take the little boat home and house her in my shed, and each spring I take the cover off and start the preparations for the coming season. And each year my father visits me, watching with stern amusement in a cloud of ghostly tobacco smoke as I retrace the steps first taken with him all those years ago. That rib is still in place, as immoveable as my memory of that day spent mending the boat.

The Opposing Escalators

My wife and I had decided to postpone having children, just for fun. That is to say, we were having too much fun to bother about babies. My mother, being a devout Catholic, never considered that contraception might be part of the plan and had convinced herself, unbeknown to us, that for whatever reason, we were unable to become parents. The tension had therefore been building for some years before that Christmas. Like the Pompeiians, my wife and I had no idea what was about to land on us as we drove to my cousin's house in Glencullen for a Christmas Eve party.

It was a gloomy December day with low clouds and day-long twilight. Cheery Christmas trees in every window did their best to brighten the gloom as we made our way up the Ballybetagh Road to the party. We were engaged in a flaming row about something. Neither of us can remember now what it was about. I had been in town that morning and festive drink was fuelling the flames on my side of the differences; it was only a polite sufficiency, but enough to ensure that it was my wife who was driving when I decided to leave the car while it was still moving, slam the door and holler at the departing vehicle that she was welcome to go to the party by herself or go to hell for all I cared. It is possible that the language had a richer texture.

I turned and headed for home, realising far too late that it was very cold, I had no overcoat with me, home was a good six miles away and that I had no keys to get in if I even managed to get there. Still, I thought, the walk would do me good, and she would be sorry when hypothermia carried me off. After some twenty minutes of striding out, my resolve was weakening, the drink was wearing off and I was getting colder and colder. The realisation that I was behaving like an idiot was of very little comfort. The lights of the city twinkled beneath me like an inverted firmament as the dim day gave up the struggle and resolved into a grateful early night. The shadows of the bosky hedgerows reminded me of a saying of my mother's that there would always be love in the world while the gorse bloomed; but it was dark, and I couldn't see any. I had just prepared a speech of high-minded self-justification when a car drew up beside me and startled me with a hoot. My wife wound down her window and said, 'Get in, you bollocks.'

In my frigid condition, this was the most welcome seasonal greeting I could have hoped for, and the best present too. The car was warm, and my high principles melted. My finely wrought speech of self-righteous vituperation, so carefully crafted and honed, evaporated, and I found myself telling my beloved that she was wonderful, and that I was a turkey.

In this bruised state, we arrived rather late at my cousin's house, abandoned the car on a grass verge and made our way to the door. As we approached, it swung open, allowing a billow of warmth, light and noise to escape with some departing revellers and allowing us to slip into the maw of the party. We sought our hostess through the mill of festive folks, most of whom were related to me to a greater or lesser degree. We became aware of an undergrowth of small children, surging and squalling around our knees, all of them overexcited, overtired and overindulged. My relations had always been enthusiastic breeders, and it appeared that the survival of the family genes had been thoroughly catered for, if not over-subscribed. Through the jungle of slightly inebriated kin and the substrata of their offspring waded my dear mother, her lovely smile shining through the fug and noise. It was clear to me that she, a sober woman, had had more than her usually modest glass of wine. Her opening gambit was delivered without forewarning, apology or explanation and with considerable hungry warmth and even the hint of a tear: 'When are you going to have one?'

Her longing for grandchildren had been rubbed raw by the friction of the children around her knees and the wine, so hospitably dispensed by my cousin's husband, whom I now saw weaving towards me, bottle in hand. I drew my tattered dignity around me.

'When we're good and ready!' I snarled and turned to wish my host a happy Christmas. I accepted a glass of wine and drank it down like a Saharan traveller arriving at an oasis.

The party was a good one. I soon forgot my upset and went to find my mother, but by this time she had left the party and was on her way home. Long before we left the party, our host had loudly and foggily wished us all a very happy Christmas and retired to his bed.

Remorse had set in on the way home, but by the time we got there, it was too late to phone my mother.

I didn't sleep well that night, constantly visited by recollections of Christmases past. I have a memory so early and yet so personal that it cannot be a given memory: I am kneeling beside my mother in the front bench of the Church of the Assumption in Dalkey on Christmas Day. Above the altar there is a large stained-glass window depicting the Assumption of the Blessed Virgin Mary; there is a lot of blue and clouds that look more like rocks on a stony beach. My mother had what was known as a special devotion to the Blessed Virgin. Through my fidgety boredom I stare up at my mother's face and see that she is looking up at the stained-glass Virgin, who herself is gazing up in ecstasy as she makes her way heavenward. Although lost in prayer, my mother's attention is somehow snagged on my stare, and she looks down at me and slowly unwraps her wondrous smile – the smile that could illuminate a room and would always light up my heart. I see such pure love pouring from that smile, the sort of love that I hoped someday to pour down on children of my own.

Wracked with sleepless contrition, early on Christmas Day I phoned my mother. She answered on the first ring and started to apologise. I gently stopped her and assured her of our love and of my regret at being short with her the night before. I told her that as far as we knew all our baby-making equipment was fully operational, and that it had been our choice to wait before setting it in motion. Later that day I cooked Christmas dinner for my wife, my parents and my in-laws. We lit candles, pulled crackers, drank wine and enjoyed the turkey.

We had babies in due course, when we were good and ready, I suppose. And my mother got Alzheimer's, for which no one can be ready. My parents would often come to our house for Sunday tea, my father valiantly covering for the expanding moth holes in my mother's memory. At the end of one of these visits, while my parents stood in the hall preparing to leave, I saw that my mother was having difficulties with the buttons on her coat. Her fingers were plucking ineffectually at the buttons, making no progress with the business of closing them. My little daughter, then aged about three, noticed too. With entirely natural grace and kindness, she reached up and helped my mother, patting each completed button and buttonhole with her little hand as she progressed, as if to bless the union. My daughter had just learned the skill of buttons, and my mother had just forgotten. They were passing each other on the opposing escalators of age.

Later, when my father had died, too exhausted from caring for my mother to fight the pneumonia that had come to take him, we looked after her until her declining condition required a nursing home. She, unaware of her surroundings, seemed blessedly serene. In time she became bedridden and immobile. Then she stopped speaking and simply lay there, eyes closed or staring at nothing.

Two days before she died, I visited her with my two little ones, then aged five and two. My mother had not spoken for months and lay in her bed with her eyes resolutely shut. She seemed to be unaware of our presence as the children perched on the end of her bed and I chattered on about the events of the day. As we got ready to leave, my mother opened her beautiful old eyes for the first time on that visit, focused on the children, unveiled her wonderful smile and said, 'Ah! The little darlings.'

She never spoke again.

New Year's Party

'We're lost, aren't we?' said my wife. She tossed the question like an unpinned hand grenade, with a barely suppressed note of triumph in her voice. Lizzie Underwood's bewildering directions to her guest house, Gort na Gaoithe, had led us down a boreen, which became a track with rushes growing in the middle, and now even that had come to an end, surrendering to nature. I stopped the car, its underbelly tickled by the rushes.

'Now what are we going to do?' This was more admonition for my stupidity than a question.

'Look, I was following Lizzie's instructions,' I said, struggling to maintain a patient tone. I slammed the car into reverse and briskly started the long journey backwards to where we had come from.

'For God's sake, you'll crash the bloody car! You're driving far too fast! Jesus! Mind the ditch!'

The tensions of the past few months erupted and I shouted back at her. 'Jesus Christ, will you let me drive the fucking car? If you want to walk, you can get out now!'

I jerked the straining car to a halt and beat the steering

wheel with both hands in a spasm of anger. Then immediately I said, 'I'm sorry, love. Sorry, sorry, sorry.' I beat the wheel again, annoyed that I had allowed hateful anger loose. 'Look,' I said in a flurry of emasculated passive-aggression. 'I really don't want to spoil our weekend, love. It's my fault for insisting on following Lizzie's directions instead of asking the way. It's a man thing. Silly of me. Sorry.'

'Oh Jesus, will you stop your meaningless apologies and turn the car. We'll ask at the next farmhouse,' she said, looking away over the sodden winter countryside.

I was in full retreat as I continued to reverse down the track until I could find a place to turn. 'I love you, sweetheart. Sorry for snapping,' I offered.

Thin-lipped silence.

Lizzie Underwood and her husband, Philip, ran a grand old guest house called Gort na Gaoithe in the heart of Westmeath. They were old friends of ours from university days, and we and a group of mutual friends had agreed to spend the New Year's holiday at their house on a paying basis, thereby boosting their business and having some fun into the bargain. We had been so looking forward to this New Year's break. In the grinding, all-consuming stress of work and children, we had been neglecting each other, and this was an opportunity to do some running repairs. On the last day of the year, we parked the kids with my wife's parents and headed west in high spirits. The last thing we needed was a quarrel.

It was afternoon, and the light was already fading by the time we found Gort na Gaoithe. The big old house sat obstinately in the flat Westmeath countryside, monument to a vanished Anglo ascendancy. Philip's Underwood forebears had rooted here after the Cromwellian campaigns. The house had been rebuilt several times, the latest dating from the 1850s. For generations, the Underwoods had enjoyed a comfortable living on the income of their tenant farmers' rents from the surrounding acres. Now the land had been sold off and the house and its family had been reduced to taking in paying guests. Although still grand, the old place looked rather too big for its boots and was beginning to sag. There were large potholes in the driveway, which resembled an assault course, and I noticed a sad little tuft of grass growing in the gutter; there was a green stain on the gable where the downpipe was leaking.

The rooks were roosting noisily in the high trees. We parked the car at the porticoed front entrance, and I pressed the silent bell. Then, after a dithering moment, I knocked. There was no answer, but the door was unlocked and slightly ajar, so we made our way tentatively through the glazed and peeling porch into the house. It seemed to be deserted. In the gathering gloom of the mid-winter afternoon, the entrance hall still exuded a lofty, if rather dilapidated grandeur: the rug was worn, but more in the way of chic distress than decay; portraits of Philip's brave soldier ancestors loomed upwards into the obscurity of the shadows; the stairs, with its run of ancient but still decent carpet, climbed mysteriously into the gloom of the upper reaches of the house. A mahogany hallstand stood sentry by the door, festooned with coats, hats and dog leads. Wellington boots sagged on the floor. We couldn't find the light switch.

'Hello,' my wife called. 'Anyone there?'

In the answering silence, I heard the patient clunking of a longcase clock in the well of the stairs. A golden retriever wandered in through the open front door, wagging its plumed tail in greeting, but none of the other inhabitants were in evidence. We investigated various doors until we found what seemed to be the drawing room. This was a fine Victorian room of gracious proportions. It was high-ceilinged with three soaring sash windows, one to the east and two to the south. The last fragments of the sunset shone ruby-yellow, lighting the ancient furnishings – a nicely assembled jumble of sway-backed, loose-covered sofas and frayed armchairs. A bookcase crowded with a mosaic of paperback and hardback books occupied the northern wall, and a fine open fireplace with a marble mantelpiece graced the eastern side. The ashy remains of a fire lay, spent and exhausted, in the grate. The air was perfumed with the incense of the previous night's woodsmoke. The December chill was creeping into the room. I began to feel rather forlorn.

'I guess we'll just have to sit and wait,' I said, sinking into one of the sofas, my overcoat still wrapped around me. My wife sank beside me, suppressing a shiver. The retriever joined us and sat on my foot companionably.

'Sorry for being cross in the car, love,' said my wonderfully forgiving wife, giving me a poke with her elbow and generously reasserting our happier mood.

Just then a young woman came into the room with a bundle of sticks and a newspaper under her arm.

'Hi there!' she greeted us cheerily as she knelt at the fireplace and started to prepare a fire.

'Um … I wonder if we could check in?' asked my wife.

'Why, is there no one around?'

'No. Perhaps you might be able to help us?' I said.

'I'm just making up a fire here. It's getting cold,' said the young woman. 'You wouldn't have any matches, would you?'

'Well, perhaps you might find another member of staff to help us,' said my wife, a righteous edge of annoyance beginning to creep into her voice.

'Oh, I don't work here. I'm a guest,' said the young woman. 'Matches?'

We blurted all sorts of apologies, and my wife found a lighter in the deeper recesses of her handbag and handed it to the young woman who applied it to the crumpled newspaper. The fire seemed disinclined to take and sulkily filled the room with smoke. We made our way wearily back to the hall, leaving the young woman in the smoke, which did not seem to bother her.

'Ahoy there!' came Lizzie's voice from the now Stygian tunnel of the back hallway. 'Welcome, welcome! Sorry if you have been waiting, but we are a bit short-handed because of the holidays. Philip is in Athlone doing some shopping for this evening's dinner. The others arrived yesterday. You missed the dance last night at the hotel. They're in the pub. Regan's. Just down the road. I'll show you to your room.'

Chatting cheerfully, Lizzie showed us up the lovely oak staircase, which swept majestically around a spacious return with another tall northern window and headed up to a sort of galleried landing supervised by a number of bedroom doors. I lugged the bags behind the women, pausing on the return to look out the window at the darkening landscape.

A sliver of moon with an attendant star was showing in a clear sky. There would be frost.

'Your room is number six,' said Lizzie, swinging the door open and turning on the light. The room was lovely. Lizzie proudly showed us the furniture, including the big brass bed, all of which had been specially commissioned for the room when the house was built. She left us to settle in and said that she would try to meet us in the pub later if she had time before dinner.

We decided to walk to the pub. The air was tight with frost and our breath showed in plumes of steamy vapour. It was very still. Stars peeped and glimmered, the moon like a fresh toenail clipping. The pub was warm and noisy. An open fire burned, adding cheer to the place. We sensed a drop in the volume of conversation as the local drinkers evaluated us. A sheepdog under a table raised its head to eye us. Christmas decorations were draped around the shelves of the bar, with fairy lights winking. A tape of Christmas songs jangled in the background. We quickly found our four friends in a corner by the fire. I ordered a pint for myself and a hot whiskey for my wife. We dragged over more chairs and joined the others at their table.

The mood among our friends seemed oddly sombre. Paul seemed to have had quite a lot to drink. His wife, Rosemary, was telling a story about their Christmas under heavy sniper fire from Paul.

'Then Paul's dad knocked over the pot with the flaming brandy in it—'

'It was whiskey, Rosemary. We always use whiskey.'

'And the flames went everywhere, all over the table. Paul's

mum grabbed Paul's jumper to smother the flames—'

'It was Dad's jacket, actually.'

'Jesus, Paul, I'm trying to tell a story about your stupid drunken family. Will you for Christ's sake stop interrupting and contradicting me!'

'Well, if you're going to tell a story about my family, at least try to get it right,' said Paul, standing to finish the last of his pint. 'Here, give us your purse there. I'm getting another drink,' and he blundered towards the bar.

John was sitting with his back to Bridget, who appeared to be engrossed with her smartphone. He was vacantly observing Paul grating at Rosemary. He was subdued and distant. When Paul asked him if he wanted a drink, he didn't reply at first, and then reacted as if he had just woken. 'Yea. Pint. Please.'

Bridget continued to ignore John altogether and barely roused herself from the fascination of her Facebook to acknowledge our arrival. Rosemary's manner was brittle, but cheery on the face of it, as she welcomed us and chatted to us about her work and the apartment that she was sharing with Paul. As she talked, my wife caught my eye and gave a small frown. She had sensed something out of kilter.

I started a conversation with John, but found that I had to work quite hard. He would start to answer my friendly questions about how he was getting on since I had last seen him, but would tend to dry up mid-sentence as if his mind was elsewhere. He volunteered little, preferring to speak only when spoken to, which was not his usual self.

The mood lifted a little when Lizzie bustled into the pub, greeting locals and shouting to the landlady for a drink, 'For the love of God, Maggie, will you pour me a pint of Guinness before I die of thirst!'

She joined my wife and Rosemary first, then came over and chatted to John and me. She seemed to be having more success with John than I had. I decided to surf on the edges of the conversation and watch.

A group of men at the counter, who had the look of long-haul drinkers, were getting increasingly loud. There was a disagreement about something and some shouting, until they were asked by the landlady to keep it down. Three of them left, all looking unsteady, but with an air of purposeful menace about them. My attention wandered back to our own party, and I was just easing into my second pint when the door of the pub burst open. A small man, looking panicked and out of breath, dashed through the bar and into the men's toilets at the back of the pub. I thought I saw blood on the side of his face. His shirt was torn. The pub door burst open again and the three men reappeared, one nursing his right hand and mumbling oaths, the others looking wildly around them in search of something or someone. One of their pals at the bar said, 'The little weasel has locked himself in the jacks,' and with a grin and a wink added, 'I think he thought there was a way out through the back.'

The three charged into the toilet, led by the man with the sore hand who roared, 'I'll kill ya, ya little fucker! Ya little fuckin' bastard.'

There was a shriek from the toilets and the sounds of blows. The landlady came out from behind the bar and strode over to the door of the toilets. She shouted through the open door, 'Quit that the lot of ye! Behave yourselves or I'll have the guards on ye. I'll not have that behaviour in this house! Out! Now!' Her voice had the sort of authority that did not expect challenge.

The three men emerged sheepishly from the gents'. The man with the sore hand tried a grin at his pals, 'That little shagger had it coming to him—'

'I said out! Right now,' commanded the landlady.

Although she only came up to his shoulder, his bravado wilted before her anger and his smile dropped. All three trooped through the pub towards the door. One of them muttered to their pals, 'We'll be in Cassidy's, lads.'

'Well wherever, ye won't be in here again. Ye are barred. Do ye hear me?'

They left, and soon their pals left too. After a pause, two local men went into the toilet and emerged with the little man between them. He was sobbing, his nose was bleeding and a large bruise had blossomed around his left eye. He could barely stand, and his helpers had to half-carry him through the pub and out the door.

All conversation in the pub had reduced to whispers. Our party sat in shocked silence. My wife was white in the face, her eyes large and her lips pale. I found that my hands were shaking and my heart seemed to beat irregularly. Only Lizzie seemed relatively at ease. She sipped her pint and provided a commentary on the happenings in an undertone.

'He's a cousin of the guy with the sore hand. The three lads are home for Christmas, and the rumour is that the little guy was riding the other guy's girlfriend while he was away. This goes on every year at this time when the emigrants come home. Old scores to settle. It's the way we do Christmas.

Let's drink up and go back to dinner. The locals don't like tourists at these events.' We finished up and left the muted pub.

Back at the house, we were greeted by Philip, who surfaced from the kitchen wearing an apron with a dishcloth hung on the cord.

'Hello all. Welcome back. Dinner is ready.' Then he turned his attention to my wife and me. 'Welcome to Gort na Gaoithe. Happy New Year. Welcome.' Philip kissed my wife on both cheeks, and he and I exchanged that brief leaning-in and back patting that seems to be required when a handshake is an insufficient expression of affection between red-blooded men. 'Would it be an imposition to ask you to give me a hand with the gravy?'

I followed him down the tunnelled hallway to the kitchen, leaving my wife and the others in the drawing room in the hands of Lizzie, who was already offering drinks as she flung an armful of logs into the fire.

As I started on the gravy, I explained to Philip something of the events we had witnessed in the pub. He gave a cynical grunt, commenting that that was typical Christmas behaviour.

'Sorry you had to witness us country folk in festive mood. And, by the way, you need to know that there was a lively difference among our own pals here last night after the dance. You missed a grand row.'

'Hmm. I was wondering about the sulky atmosphere. Paul and Rosemary are bickering, and John and Bridget aren't talking.'

'Well, from what I picked up last night, Bridget caught John misbehaving with one of our other guests back here after the dance. According to what she shouted at him at four this morning, Bridget had found the pair of them unzipped and urgent in the butler's pantry. She's chucked him out of the conjugal romper room. He slept in a chair on the landing. And it's the usual stuff with Rosemary and Paul: they're tearing the tripes out of each other– normal service. A nice mess.'

I managed to make lumpy gravy, but Philip assured me that it was good enough for 'the grumpies', as he called them, and we brought the dinner through to the dining room, with Philip hollering to all that dinner was served.

Dinner was a subdued affair and, although Philip made sure that the wine flowed freely, unfortunately the conversation remained congealed. I was beside Lizzie, who pretended to flirt with me all through dinner in a very flattering way. My wife was between John and Philip, and although I could see her doing her best to engage John in something like a conversation, she eventually gave up and allowed herself to be entertained solely by Philip's chatter. Rosemary sipped her water coldly as Paul gulped his wine and contradicted everything she ventured. Bridget made polite small talk but seemed to be pining for her phone.

Just before midnight Philip produced two bottles of Champagne. The corks popped like silenced pistol shots. Philip handed round glasses of the bubbling wine. We turned on the radio to catch the midnight stroke, and on the hour we wished ourselves a happy New Year and drank a toast to auld lang syne.

Just then the dining-room door opened and the smoky-fire-lighting female guest peeped in to wish us all a happy

New Year and good night. When she shut the door, Bridget turned to John, 'Aren't you going to join your little friend? Finish what you were at last night?'

'Shut up, Bridget, for God's sake,' John said.

'That hooer has a right nerve to show her face in here. And you are good enough for her.'

John stood and pushed back his chair. 'Ah fuck this, I'm going back to the pub. Sorry, guys,' he said and left the room, shutting the door briskly behind him.

'My door will be locked if you ever come back, you prick,' Bridget shouted after him.

My wife whispered to me, 'For God's sake, let's sneak off to bed. This is too dreary.' And as soon as decency would allow, we bade everyone a good night and climbed the stairs to No. 6.

I am happy to say that, snuggled under the duvet in that very musical brass bed, we ushered in the New Year in proper fashion, so grateful that we had not been infected by the squabbles and horrors of the day. We were grateful for our love – I astonished by its constancy, my wife, as always, brimming with generous affection, bundling her love at me as if it were to be expected. The jingles of the bed and the dyspeptic gurglings of the ancient central-heating system mixed to provide, it seemed to us, a perfect soundtrack for a New Year celebration.

Next morning, the first day of the year, we woke to frosted windows and frigid air mixed with warm, moist updraughts from the valiant old radiator. We were alone in the dining room for breakfast. There was no sign of our hosts or our other friends. We ate the enormous breakfast that was put before us by an impossibly timid young local girl, who was so tongue-tied with shyness that she was effectively dumb. Then we ventured outside where the world had been transformed overnight into a delicately beautiful icescape. The heavy frost and light sprinkling of snow had covered everything in a sparkling of white hoar. Icicles spiked from the gutters, and even the phone lines were dusted with ice. The sky was a clear pale blue and the sun had just made an entrance, lighting the world aslant with an orange glow that had, as yet, no warmth.

'It's so lovely,' my wife murmured, 'I don't want the sun to melt it.'

I felt my love for my wife warm within me like the embers of a turf fire banked and damped to survive the night. And this emotion brought with it a strange feeling of guilt. As I walked with her, arm in arm on this breathless winter morning, I wondered what I had done to deserve her continued love, and what it was within my own inner tangle that allowed a straight thread of devotion for her to have developed and prospered. Why had I, why had we, been so fortunate as to find ourselves playing out our marriage vows of constant love while our friends seemed to find only discord and unhappiness? I felt the guilt of the survivor: a soldier left standing when his comrades had fallen, or a lucky passenger pulled alive from a train wreck. I was afraid to voice any of this lest I broke the spell – like a wish made on some pishogue that won't be granted if you tell it to anyone.

We found a way down to the nearby lake and stood at the water's edge, our breath in clouds around us. A thin layer of ice had collected at the lakeshore and the reeds were dusted with a sparkling of frost. Smoky wisps of vapour hung over the water. A bickering of moorhens set up nearby, filling the otherwise suspended soundscape. My wife leant against me. I was overcome by a wave of pure happiness.

Rather than tempt luck, we hurried back to the house, grabbed our bags, stole a sheet of notepaper and left a note of thanks and apology on the hallstand. We paid the mute-shy girl and fled the scene. We drove home to Dublin in silence, each lost in our own thoughts, to face a New Year.

This Is Supposed to Be Fun

I have always been a slave to the Yuletide thing. It is something that I have inherited, and I have taken elaborate care to ensure that the habit of subservience to every aspect of the tradition gets passed on to my own children – cards, carols, crib, and church; holly, mistletoe, tree and candle; turkey, ham, mince pies and presents; Santa Claus, reindeer, sleigh and bells – the whole shooting gallery.

My wife and I had duly brainwashed our children to believe in the myth of Santa Claus, and we encouraged them to write letters of demand addressed to this jolly old fiction and put them up the sitting-room chimney. The parent of a guest at my eldest son's fifth birthday party in October had splurged at the Two Euro shop and given him a present of a gimcrack toy that shot out little plastic discs, which immediately got lost or were eaten by the dog. The toy had soon been stood on and destroyed, probably by me, and of course a replacement was the first item on my son's list of desires in his letter to Santa. I was dispatched to find the replacement disc-shooter. I spent a frustrating and fruitless week of lunchtimes scouring every toy shop and bargain basement in Dublin, but nothing even faintly matching the stupid toy could I find. As I entered the second week of my hunt, the matter had become an obsession and was beginning to interfere with my sleep pattern at work. I had eliminated every low-price shop within a two-mile radius of my workplace, and I was beginning to explore the bargain shops slightly further afield, straying ultimately as far as the North Side. It was in a shop in Parnell Street that I finally ran the elusive toy to earth. In an ecstasy of joy, I carried my prize to the cash desk, tears of relief and fulfilment flowing freely. I paid the puzzled Chinese lady and went on my exultant way back to my office in such a state of elation that I was unable to do any work that afternoon. The disc-shooter in my son's stocking would reinforce his belief in Father Christmas.

My wife and I made a mistake in our early years of parenthood. We adhered to the idiotic notion that Santa Claus left each child's Christmas stocking at the foot of their bed, rather than the less personalised delivery under the tree in the sitting room. This is a lovely romance, and it must be conceded that nothing, and I mean NOTHING, can match the thrill and excitement of the feel of a bulging Christmas stocking discovered before first light. But, as our children grew older and more excitable, we found that the romance was counterbalanced by the fact that the brats could not, or would not, go to sleep on Christmas Eve. This meant that Santa Claus' visit to our house had to be delayed until later and later in the night, and eventually into the early hours, as we waited for our children to pass out from exhaustion; then, and only then, could the stockings be delivered without fear of discovery. In the year of the disc-shooter, the stockings had been carefully stuffed with all sorts of gewgaws (not forgetting the orange and the banana in the toe) including a toy cat for my daughter that mewed when squeezed and the wretched, hard-won disc-shooter for my eldest son. Our youngest son was only eighteen months and mercifully ignorant of the lies and deception that were being practised on his older siblings by his loving parents.

The filled stockings were hidden under the stairs. We retired for the night at about eleven o'clock, with our three children still very much awake but dutifully in their beds awaiting the arrival of Santa Claus and his sleigh. The first to break rank was my seven-year-old daughter, who stumped in to our bedroom at about midnight, announcing that she couldn't sleep. I brought her back to her own bed twice, but I could see that hysteria was threatening, so we gave in and brought her in to our bed. After an hour of relentless kicking and thrashing, I had had enough and excused myself to doss down in my daughter's now vacant bed. She shared a room with my eldest son, who had been woken by all the nomadic behaviour, and he demanded to be allowed to sleep in the bed with my wife and daughter. This seemed to me to be a good idea, offering, as it did, some prospect of sleep for me. My wife, however, found it impossible to survive for any length of time with the two eldest children in the bed with her, and soon she wandered in to take up the vacancy in my son's bed. Our youngest, never a great sleeper at the best of times, decided that it was time to get in on the act, and he started to cry at about one in the morning. I was instructed to go and offer him solace. We had a futon and a duvet in his room for occasions such as this. I unrolled the futon and spread myself and my youngest thereupon, drawing the duvet over us both. This arrangement lasted about an hour, during which the two older children had grown lonesome and had wandered back to their own room in search of a parent or two. At about half past two in the morning, my youngest woke again and became inconsolable for want of his mother. My wife emerged from the children's bedroom and took possession of the infant. Not being sure of who was sleeping where at this stage, I took myself off to the spare room, where I think I managed all of an hour of fitful sleep before my wife appeared in the doorway, in tears with exhaustion.

'This is supposed to be fucking fun,' she sobbed, as she hunkered in the corner.

'Happy Christmas,' I offered, and we both started to laugh in a manner that was only a sleigh-bell's tinkle away from full-blown madness.

We took up temporary residence in the spare-room bed together and waited for another thirty minutes. All seemed quiet. We tiptoed downstairs and got the stockings. On the way back up the stairs, my grip on one of the over-stuffed stockings slipped and I had to grab at it to stop it falling. It emitted a high-pitched mewing noise. It was the stocking intended for my daughter, and I had squeezed the toy cat, which did exactly what it was supposed to do. We froze halfway up the stairs, sure that the mewing would wake everyone in the house. The toy had been well made; when squeezed, it miaowed not once, not twice, but three times. Nothing would quiet the thing once it had started its feline song. Any attempt to stifle the noise was likely to produce another round of mewing. All we could do was stand there in the dark and the cold, choking back our giggles until the tears came, waiting for the wretched toy to shut up and praying to whatever deranged God had placed us in this absurdity, that the children would remain asleep. By some weird miracle our prayer was answered, and all three slept through the caterwauling. They continued to sleep as we crept into their rooms and delivered Santa's bounty carefully at the foot of each bed, then retired to our own chamber, exhausted. And there we lay, unable to sleep, despite the gnawing exhaustion that was consuming both of us. We were too hyper, too excited, too fizzed up. All we could do was lie there and wait sleeplessly for Santa Claus. It didn't take long. By five o'clock in the morning Christmas Day was in full swing, and there was no stopping it, sleep or no sleep.

My eldest son overlooked the damned disc-shooter completely in favour of another cheap plastic toy that had been crammed into his stocking with no care or forethought whatsoever. I could not, for fear of frightening away the spirit of Santa, tell my son what trouble I had gone to to find the shooter. But I found that a large gin and tonic after Mass that morning restored my own spirits extremely well, and our Christmas, that year, turned out to be fun after all.

Something Unresolved

My daughter was in senior infants with a little girl who came from a family of born-again bigots, who believed that if a person did not believe in their fundamentalist Christian vision of God and creation, that person was doomed to hell. It was therefore probably intended as an act of kindness that, late in June that year, the little girl from the born-again family decided to inform my daughter that Santa Claus didn't exist, and that all the wonderful Christmas presents actually came from her parents. The news did not go down well.

My wife collected a very troubled six-year-old daughter from school that day and spent most of the afternoon trying to find out what the problem was. It was like cracking a safe. Every angle was explored.

'Why are you crying, love?'

'Cos I'm sad.'

'What's made you so sad, pet?'

'Nothing.'

'If it was nothing you wouldn't be upset. What happened? Was someone mean to you?'

'No.'

'Did someone do something to you that you didn't like?'

'Just leave me alone!'

'But I want to make it better. I can't do that by leaving it alone, can I? What's up, darling? Tell Mummy. Was Teacher cross?'

'No. I'm OK. Just leave me alone.' She sat on the bottom step of the stairs with her arm around the dog.

By the time I got home from work, my wife's interrogation was beginning to bear fruit, and our daughter was beginning to open up a bit. But, of course, my arrival set things back a step, and the child had to be allowed a bit of space before the questioning began again.

'Go out and cut the grass,' I was told.

'But it doesn't need cutting.'

'Well it won't take so long then, will it? Out!'

'But I'm just home!'

'Yes, and now you are going to cut the grass. Try not to be stupid and just do as I say!'

A bewildered gardener started the mower and set about the grass, trying, in accordance with his instructions, not to be stupid.

The previous Easter, we had decided to take a holiday in the Canary Islands. It was our first time to venture overseas with all three children, so it was something of a step into the unknown. Our flight to Lanzarote was scheduled to depart at six o'clock in the morning of Good Friday. We had to be at the airport two hours before departure, so we decided to leave home at 2.30 a.m. at the latest. We had intended going to bed early, but the need to check the expiry date on the passports, to unpack and repack all the bags to make sure that my wife's spare swimsuit hadn't been forgotten and, finally, to ensure the Easter Bunny's eggs were stowed somewhere they would not break, be discovered, melt or get stolen, meant that we finally settled down at about two o'clock. We had just closed our eyes when the alarm went off to signal the start of our Easter holidays. My eyes felt like someone had been sandpapering them during my brief rest, and my stomach was in full revolt, crying 'hunger' on the one hand and 'nausea' on the other. Our three children were relative exemplars of good behaviour. The older pair had slept fairly well, but our youngest, who was only two, hadn't. This wasn't unusual for him. He was causing a ruckus about wanting to wear his wellingtons and refused point-blank to put on his sandals. I was trying not to react with imbecile tetchiness to my wife's obsessive compulsion to check everything four times and to ask me again and again if I had packed the diarrhoea pills.

After an impromptu exploration of parts of Finglas and Ballymun that I never wish to see again, we eventually found the long-term car park. The charge for the parking was more expensive than the cost of the flight. It included a courtesy shuttle bus, which promised to depart the car park every ten minutes. We waited in frigid pre-dawn conditions for twenty-five minutes for the bus, and its surly driver, that duly lurched and bounced us to the departure terminal. Having retrieved our luggage from the belly of the bus, we threw ourselves and our children into the teeming maelstrom of the departure hall. We battled our way to our check-in queue, where we stood in line like bad-tempered zombies for nearly half an hour while the Ryanair person conducted a long and animated telephone conversation with her mother in Poland. Finally, after a powerful string of invective in Polish, she slammed the phone down and crankily opened up the desk. My nerves were flayed raw from lack of sleep and the repeated rush and withdrawal of adrenalin that always seems to go with airport visits. The person in the queue behind me liked to chivvy me along by banging the backs of my calves with their luggage trolley. After the fourth time this happened, I turned angrily to remonstrate with my assailant and found myself facing a six-foot-five-inch, twenty-five-stone gentleman with a shaven head and an array of very tasteful tattoos covering his arms as far up as his singlet vest would reveal. His fists were inscribed respectively 'LOVE' and 'ATE' (the 'H' of HATE was covered by a grubby piece of Elastoplast). He had another tattoo on his throat, depicting a dotted line with the words 'CUT HERE'.

'How are you doing?' I mumbled, trying to turn my angry snarl into a meek smile in one seamless movement. He made no reply, but nonchalantly crashed his trolley again into my legs, this time catching my shins.

I was disconcerted to note that the same gentleman and his extended family were seated behind us on the airplane. I envisaged a troublesome flight ahead, and I was not let down. My youngest decided that flying disagreed with his ears. His high-pitched vocal objection to the pressure imbalance between his inner ears and the plane's cabin pressure strongly disagreed with my ears, and I decided that movement and distraction might help, so for most of the three-hour journey I promenaded up and down the aisle with my shrieking, wellington-wearing, infant son in my arms.

I apologised to Mr Tattoo. 'Sorry about this.'

'No worries, pal.' But soon his patience was exhausted. 'For fuck's sake will ya quiet that child!'

'I'm sorry, but there's nothing I can do.'

'Fuckin' well give him a box in the head! That'd sort his problems.' He rose in his seat, as if to demonstrate his suggested cure, but had overlooked his seatbelt, which had, in accordance with in-flight safety instructions, remained fastened. His floundering battle with his restraining belt caused his large belly to rise, moon-like, from his seat, tilting his table and folding it into the seat in front of him, spilling his drink all over his brand-new XXL white Nike tracksuit pants and runners. Rum and Coke will stain if not treated immediately, I thought, but kept this domestic advice to myself. The spillage certainly took his mind off the noise being made by my son, and I was soon out of immediate range of his indelibly decorated fists. He was asleep in his seat, and my son was likewise snoozing in my arms, by the time I had finished my tour of the airplane. I decided to do a lap of honour rather than risk disturbing either gentleman.

Our ground-floor apartment at Puerto del Carmen was lovely, once we had beaten the six-inch centipede to death with a flip-flop and had obtained from reception, and deployed, an anti-ant aerosol so full of toxins that we have probably, in that single act of insecticide, rung the death knell of the entire planet. We settled in when the fumes and the ants had died down, and I had removed the carcass of the many-legged intruder.

I rose at dawn on Easter Sunday and carefully hid the Easter Eggs in the hibiscus hedge just outside our front door.

After breakfast, my wife kicked off the proceedings.

'I wonder if the Easter Bunny has been?'

'The Easter Bunny? But we're not at home, Mummy!'

'Oh, you can't be sure with the Bunny. He may have found us. Will we go and see?'

A clamorous stampede for the front door followed, and the next twenty minutes were spent ransacking the hedge for the Easter Bunny's bounty. The children responded to our guidance of 'Getting cold now … Warmer … Warmer … WARMER! RED HOT!' and shrieked with delight as each foil-wrapped confection was discovered. All things considered, the Feast of the Resurrection of Christ went very well in our temporary household, even to the extent that there were no tears when the children were introduced to the concept of rationing: not being allowed to devour all of the chocolate at a single sitting.

At the end of our holiday, my wife and I were completely exhausted from concentrated parenting, and we were glad to get back to the uncertainties of April in Ireland and the measured routine of school, work and domestic life. And this nicely predictable pattern continued in its measured pace until that June afternoon when our daughter came home with her shattering news about Santa Claus.

The lawn did not require mowing, but I went through the motions, absenting myself, as instructed, from the tensions of my wife's interrogation of our daughter. It was just as I came back in to the house that she cracked.

'Lisa says that Santa isn't real. She says her mummy said that the mummies and daddies just pretend.' Big tears welled in our little girl's beautiful blue eyes as her lower lip quivered.

How dare Lisa's mummy inflict this on our child; no wonder they threw Christians to the lions, I thought.

'But how could Mummy and Daddy deliver presents to all the children in the world on Christmas Eve?' My valiant wife was determined to avoid straight lies and adopted evasive questioning instead.

I added, 'And Daddy could never get down our chimney.' Which was certainly true.

'But Lisa said ...' and now the tears were in full spate.

'Well if Lisa and her mummy and daddy don't believe in Santa, then he doesn't have to come to them at Christmas,' said my clever wife.

'But she said her mummy said Santa wasn't real.'

I was worried now. I plunged in with, 'Well, I believe in Santa Claus! If you don't believe in him he mightn't come!'

But my wife, always a superior tactician, had decided on a diversion. And like all good generals she was prepared to sacrifice some of her troops in the cause of victory.

'Well, darling, we've got a little confession to make,' she said, taking her daughter's hands in hers.

I stopped breathing. What was she at? My little girl was sobbing, nearly inconsolable.

'Will I tell you, love?'

'What?' It was clear that our little one did not want to hear the answer.

'Well, you know the Easter Bunny?'

An imperceptible nod as she allowed herself to be sidetracked.

'Well, that *is* Mummy and Daddy. The Bunny is only a bit of fun for the very little ones.'

My daughter stared at her mother. She forgot her tears as she digested this bit of intelligence.

My breathing resumed, and I gazed at my wife in awed wonder. What a clever piece of psychology. By murdering the Easter Bunny, she had achieved two things: she had completely distracted our daughter from the Santa issue, and at the same time she had given the little girl some high ground from which she could look down on her two younger brothers. Masterful.

We were silent for a while, parents absorbing their complicity in the Bunny Conspiracy and daughter computing the rationale in her very young brain while at the same time mourning the demise of the Bunny.

'But Mummy?'

'What, love?'

'Last Easter in Lanzarote, the Easter Bunny was real then, wasn't he?'

Hey, Blondie!

It is the summer of 2007. The air in Bray South is throbbing with the sound of aircraft and rancid with pollen and hormones. My youngest has just turned fourteen, with all the world-weary ennui of a battle veteran. He has a shrug to answer every question, evasions to counter all interrogations and attitude enough to fuel a world revolution. He has discovered that the most effective way to enrage his mother is to adopt a sulky silence and an aggressive indifference to everything he knows she values. I skirt the war zone carefully, knowing that any intervention is likely to bring both sides down on me.

My son has celebrated the start of his school holidays by dyeing his hair in bright yellow blotches, so that he looks rather like a tie-dyed hyena. He is oblivious or perhaps indifferent to the point of aggression on the topic of his appearance. His mother has tried in vain to help with his coiffure but has been rejected with the full blast of a fourteen-year-old's scorn, leaving her helpless and bewildered. However, she retains sufficient strength to pass the problem to me, pointing out with, I feel, unwarranted venom that it's my task as his father to take the boy in hand. This baton is firmly and decidedly passed to me as the last man in the sprint team, but I already feel out of breath before I leave my mark. What am I supposed to say to him?

'Are you sure the hair was a good idea?'

'No. I fuckin' hate it. But it's too late now.'

'Mum could dye it your natural colour again.'

'That is so gay.'

'There is nothing gay about that.'

'You guys are such fuckin' losers.'

He times his exit with precision, narrowly missing an explosion of sudden violence from his father, who feels like a badger cornered by a particularly stroppy, bad-mannered bull terrier.

My wife decides (with economic lack of reference to me) that we need to spend some quality time with our son, and with an exhausted cheeriness resembling the last intense blaze of a bulb that is about to fail, she makes an offer.

'Would you like to come with us to the air show in Bray this afternoon?'

My son shows no outward sign of having heard or registered this invitation. He simply puts down the half-finished bowl of cereal that he has been slurping and lumbers out of the kitchen.

'You shouldn't let him treat us like that. Speak to him. Now!'

I lumber after my lumbering son.

It is mid-July. The day has dawned fine. Warm sunshine has made an unlikely entrance, having unaccountably been delayed in the wings while the rest of nature waited cold and wet in a summer that has been relentlessly overcast and frigid. The birds make a fuss over it by singing loudly. The small flies and midges, which have been keeping their heads down since before the end of the last ice age, have burst out of their chrysalises, eggs, nests or wherever it is that these creatures doze through the colder months, and hover and shimmy in the air. Swallows circle and dive, their shrill cries telling the world that summer has arrived and encouraging all to make the most of it. And, above the swallows, a droning biplane makes a lazy circle in the cloudless sky.

My parental toolkit is sadly wanting in the essentials for dealing with almost every situation. I tell myself to try to avoid unnecessary confrontation, to try to pick my battles carefully, to try not to descend to the level of the adolescent and to play for time. I catch up with my son in his evil-smelling bedroom, but before I can open negotiations, I am pre-empted.

'Dad, can I have twenty euros?' He offers no eye contact.

'What for?'

'Cos I need it.'

'Yes, but what for?'

'I'm gettin' my nose pierced.'

My breathing becomes slightly laboured. 'Have you asked your mother?' This is a cunning play for time, and I pray she can't hear me.

'Why? Can you not give me twenty euros?'

I stay calm. I stay cool and reasoning. 'No. About your nose—'

'Why? Are you not capable of making a decision on your own?'

My breathing is now seriously impaired, and my blood pressure is rising. 'Don't be cheeky,' I snap.

'Why is it cheeky to ask for twenty euros?'

'I said not to be cheeky!' The red mist is forming.

'Look, there's no need to be a narky shite just because you can't make a fuckin' decision.'

The red mist descends. 'Don't speak to you father like that, you little shit.' And there it is: the red mist now fully obscures any cognitive function, and I abandon all effort at being adult.

'Oh, I'm a little shit, am I? And you're supposed to be my father? Fuckin' useless family.'

'No, you can't have twenty bloody euro, and you can't have your bloody nose pierced!' My parental decision is announced in a near-scream.

'Doin' it anyway. You can't stop me. Fuckin' useless fuckin' father.' Again, he leaves the room just a hair's breadth before I obliterate him and exchange parenthood for the far easier conditions offered by a term of life imprisonment.

The sky is still throbbing to the sound of many aircraft as they hover, circle and hold formation for the Bray Air Show which is scheduled for half past two this afternoon. After consultation with my wife, and a glass of cold water, I agree to a second sally with the olive branch. I find him playing 'Grand Theft Auto' with the curtains drawn and all the windows shut. I wait until he has reversed over the lady with the pram.

'Come on with us to the air show. It'll be fun.'

'No. Goin' out.'

I mustn't take offence. I withdraw the hand of parental

friendship before it is severely mauled. 'Where?' I ask. He's fourteen. This is a reasonable question, isn't it?

'Out.'

'Who with?'

'Friends.'

'Which friends?' I absolutely must stay focused and breathe.

'Friends.'

'WHICH FRIENDS?' As I teeter on the precipice once again, I wonder who the patron saint of parents of adolescents is and decide he or she needs to step up to the mark and do something to justify their sacred rank.

'Just because you don't have any friends in your lame life doesn't mean that I have to go to a gay air show with you.'

'Well your mother and I are going. Do you want a lift as far as Bray?' I conclude that the patron saint must have been a martyr.

And so the three of us get into the car and set off for Bray. The rest of the world has had the same idea, and every conveyance capable of moving is attempting to reach Bray seafront for the funfair and the air show. The unfamiliar sun beats down on the roofs of many cars and reflects in glaring glitter off windscreens and mirrors. Windows are wound down, radios are playing and there is a strange sort of holiday tension in the air – just the tranquil side of road-rage – as the traffic eventually comes to a standstill. We abandon the car with two wheels perched illegally on the pavement and proceed on foot. My wife and I exchange views in a lively way on the subject of parking tickets and the likelihood thereof. My point, which I think is well made, is that if she wants to find a better place to park, she can do it on her own.

Our offspring, having announced that he didn't ask to be born and that it is his right in this free country to walk where he likes, has decided that he will walk ten paces in front of us, thus avoiding the embarrassment of any misunderstanding that he might be in some way associated with us. He walks with a certain jaunt in his step, his backpack slung negligently on one shoulder, the crotch of his jeans, in the fashion of the day, barely clearing his knees. And in this odd crocodile we progress down the Killarney Road and onto Bray's main street. At this point we join what appears to be the whole population of the east coast of Ireland: harassed parents with howling children clutching melting ice-creams in prams and buggies; their demented grandparents on Zimmer frames and a pack of untrained Rottweilers, slobbering and defecating all over the crowded pavement. Progress through Bray is slow and messy.

We turn off the main street onto Quinnsboro Road and saunter along in the sunshine between the high façades of the once grand Victorian terraces and the plane trees that line the boulevard. We pretend to take no notice of the sadly large assortment of winos and drug addicts who have taken up station at every bench and low wall to share their cans and to address the world in loud and inarticulate language on the subject of the inequities of life. A gentleman in a torn anorak with something unspeakable spilt down the front of his tracksuit, and something wholly unmentionable staining the back of his low-slung britches, lurches out in front of us and stands in a wobblesome way, as if trying to decide whether to fall over or launch himself into a sprint. Gravity decides matters on his behalf, and he sits in the middle of the road as my wife and I step primly around him.

About halfway down Quinnsboro Road, still preceded by our disassociated son, we find that a bevy of juvenile females, Bray's finest, have fallen into step behind us. They are dressed as if for a disco: transparent tops showing black brassieres; hair impossibly backcombed, gelled and lacquered; skirts so short that one felt sure that their mothers could not have seen them leave, and complexions more orange than the Twelfth of July. Gum is being chewed and popped and cigarettes hungrily puffed as they strut along in their stilt platform shoes. We ignore them of course. Then we hear the voice of one of these females.

'Hey, blondie!'

We pay no attention, naturally.

'Hey, blondie. You with the backpack!'

We pay even less attention.

'Hey, you with the jeans!'

To our intense mortification, we realise that the voice is aimed at our youngest, still jaunting along ten paces in front of us. He seems to be paying even less attention than we are.

'Hey, blondie in the jeans with the backpack! I'd *ride* you!'

Did the tips of his ears go pink, or was that a trick of the light? Mercifully we have reached the train station, where our son is due to take a train to Dun Laoghaire. We cross the tracks at the level crossing and make our way to the crowded and noisy esplanade. The coastguard helicopter is performing gyrations over the sea as an RNLI crew stages a mini shipwreck for the entertainment of the good people of Bray. A jet screams overhead, trailing green smoke. Our attention is distracted from the departure of our boy and from the ribaldry of his admirer.

As we find a place where we can sit in the sun and enjoy a cool drink while watching the overhead aeronautics, we replay the vignette over and over again, laughing at our son's apparent cool and the cheerful brassiness of the young one with her lewd taunts and teasing. My wife pretends to be affronted, but I know that she can't help feeling proud to be the mother of the focus of this adolescent attention. I confess to my own pride in being his father and I order drinks.

But there is another slightly disturbing dimension to this that lurks just beyond the periphery of my cognisance.

Then it dawns on me.

I feel jealous.

A Nice Surprise

My wife and I had not spoken for more than an hour. We sat in tense silence as the road unwound in front of us. We had come from Ireland on a holiday to the American Midwest: a road trip from Chicago to Memphis and back. And now we had bickered and picked our way into a fight that left me drained and depressed.

I drove the car in the late-spring rain up the steep dirt trail through the woods, following the signs that pointed to the reception building of Pine Ridge Log Cabins. It had been my idea to spend some days self-catering in the backwoods. I had chosen and booked this destination online, lured by its promise of old-time Kentucky authenticity. The car splashed into the muddy yard. There was a broken refrigerated display cabinet rusting in a corner with some other junk and an exhausted-looking pickup truck parked by the door to what might have been the reception building. A big mongrel dog on a chain barked at us. After some time, a tall bearded man in his forties emerged from the dark of one of the outbuildings. He was wearing faded army fatigues and big laced boots. His hair was in a tight crew cut under a baseball cap, which he wore with the peak at the back. He greeted us, introduced himself as Jim and asked what he could do for us folks. His large belly strained against his clothes. He stood in the rain, tucking and retucking his shirt into the waist of his trousers. I told him that we had booked a cabin by email and he went to the office in search of our paperwork. He came out again wearing a rainproof jacket and checked our details on a clipboard. He lit a cigarette.

'This is our first season here,' he said, the cigarette in one corner of his mouth. 'I've recently left the military, and me and my wife, Jen, bought this spread about a year ago.' He scanned the untidy yard without enthusiasm. 'I was honourably discharged for medical reasons …' he added, turning back to us, his voice trailing off.

I asked if he had served overseas.

'No, sir. I served at a base in Texas. That's where I met Jen. She was an army nurse. She's gone civilian now. Works in Paducah. We have a son, Tim. He's at grade school.'

Jim ground the stub of his cigarette into the mud of the yard and told us that he would get the key for our cabin if we would excuse him for a moment. We looked around at the dripping trees and the puddled trails that led, unsigned, to unknown parts of Pine Ridge. From a pasture below us on the hill, a horse whinnied. A slight brightening to the east suggested that the rain might lift. Jim started the pickup and jounced out of the yard. We followed him a short distance down a dirt road. He pulled up outside a wooden cabin that reminded me of a large garden shed.

The trees towered over our cabin and crowded around it as if jealous of its space. The light, greenish and gloomy, filtered through the leaves above. The track was rutted from winter storm run-offs. A circle of rocks formed a firepit in the space just down the hill from the cabin. The rain dripped through the leaf canopy. Mosses grew. Old railroad sleepers retained a terraced parking area by the cabin. There was a roofed stoop at the front of the cabin with two rocking chairs and a view through the trees to the pasture and its horse. In the distance we could see a small road weave its way from somewhere to somewhere else. Birds twittered to one another dejectedly and the rain dripped.

Jim opened the door of the cabin with a defeated sort of flourish and told us that this was our home for the next two days. The living room was so dark that he had to turn on the light. The light somehow made the room seem darker. He also switched on the overhead fan, which whirled above us, agitating the exhausted air as he showed us round. Jim apologised that the bed linen had not yet been changed and that fresh towels had not been put in the bathroom.

I could tell that my wife was not happy with the cabin. I too had expected better. However, we were both bruised from our recent spat and each too travel-worn to risk upsetting the other by saying anything. Neither of us had the energy to complain. We told Jim that it was fine. Jim left, telling us that Jen would be back from her work in an hour and that she would arrange for fresh linen on the bed and for the bathroom to be cleaned. Jim's job was clearly in front-of-house, while Jen did the heavy lifting. Maybe his medical condition didn't allow him to change sheets or wield the bleach bottle.

We unpacked our suitcases and put our water in the fridge. The bedside clock radio kept up a cheerful chatter in the background. Its tuner was stuck on the local country music radio station and refused to move. The volume control was also broken, so the sound was either very loud or silent. We allowed the country music and the local advertising wash around us as a balm to our battle scars. It was all part of being in America.

'I'm sorry, love,' I said.

'You always overreact.'

'You yelled at me for taking the wrong turn. I didn't do it on purpose.'

'You said you'd slap me if I yelled again.'

'You know I didn't mean that. I'd never raise my hand to you. I never have and never will. When you yell at me it makes me angry. I never yell at you like that. I overreacted.'

'It's always all about you, isn't it? You're always the centre of your universe.'

'Well, I'm the one you were yelling at.'

'I just yelled, OK? You always take it so personally.'

'Hey, let's leave it alone. I'm really sorry for my part in it. I don't want to fight with you on our holidays.'

A tense and silent truce descended. A girl's voice on the radio sang 'Mind your own biscuits and life will be gravy.' A pedal steel guitar wailed.

In due course Jen arrived, full of apologies that she had not been there to greet us. She explained that she'd had to pick up her son from school after work, and then she had to do the grocery shopping and visit the sheriff's office about some hunting-licence issues. She changed the bed sheets, cleaned the bathroom and put out fresh towels.

Jen was blonde, overweight and jolly. A long rope-like

plait hung down between her shoulder blades. She liked to talk. Her Paducah drawl was warm and rich, like honey flowing off a spoon. She told us that the next cabin to ours had been rented for two nights by a man from Memphis as a special surprise for his wife, and that the couple were to arrive the following evening and stay for two days.

'Such a nice surprise,' Jen said.

We asked her where we could buy some fresh food.

'There's Whaleys, about five miles down the road, but you don't want to go there. Nope, you want the Food Market on the other side of town.' Jen gave us detailed directions which neither of us could follow. Then she left and we set off to try to find the Food Market.

We drove past low wooden buildings on either side of the road, each with a flagpole complete with the Stars and Stripes hanging sodden, limp and forlorn. We eventually found the Food Market but could not find anything that looked edible by way of fresh food among aisle after aisle of frozen and processed products. At the back of the store was a large display-counter offering guns of every size and description, from handguns to automatic rifles. I wondered if we were expected to shoot our dinner.

Back at the cabin with our groceries, I fired up the barbeque, opened a bottle of beer and fixed my wife a drink. The clock radio was playing sad country songs about broken relationships and drinking. I don't know whether it was the sentimental music or the sodden atmosphere of the woods in the rain, but I felt my mood dip. I must have allowed a sigh to escape. My wife asked if I was OK, and I shrugged her off. She tried to keep things light, swimming for both of us against the undertow of my mood swing. Privately, I wondered if the holiday had been a good idea and whether I could trust myself not to contaminate my wife's spirits with my own gloom.

'That bug spray is a planet killer. Have you read the can?' she asked.

'Mosquitos always go for me. I have to use something,' I said, fighting the urge to be surly.

'Well you can take a shower before you come to bed. You smell like a toxic dump.'

The hot dogs were edible, without being appetising, as were the oven-cook French fries and the boil-in-the-bag peas.

'This is wilderness living at its best,' said my wife, her wryness adding spice to the tasteless meal.

I tried to light a fire in the firepit, but all the firewood was too wet and I succeeded only in producing dense clouds of choking smoke. Darkness arrived, and in the gloom we saw fireflies dance and heard an owl call. A moon showed between the trees. We sat on the stoop on our rocking chairs and thought about America.

For whatever reason, we both slept badly that night. Next morning we drove again through the rain to the small local town and wandered around. Main Street looked as if it had successfully resisted change for more than a century. Almost in a projection of my thoughts, I heard horses' hooves and then saw a small, black horse-drawn buggy swing into the street. At the reins was a man in a wide-brimmed hat, black suit and a collarless shirt. He had a long beard and his hair was in a sort of bob that looked as if someone had cut it at the kitchen table. Beside him on the bench was a young woman in long grey woollen clothes and a bonnet. Her face was pale, but perhaps that was because she was wearing no make-up. She looked like a novice nun.

'Amish,' said my wife.

We watched the buggy move at a trot down Main Street, its battery-operated rear lights strangely anachronistic. There was an unseasonable chill in the air. My self-absorbed, angry mood dip still lurked like a migraine or a stalker in the shadows. We stopped for coffee at a small diner on the hill. There was a warmth and a homeliness to the place that I found soothing. I felt my blues begin to melt. The stout waitress canted onto one hip as she took our order and told us, in her beautiful Midwest drawl, that our accents were divine.

We sipped our coffees.

'I can sort of understand the Amish mentality,' I said to my wife, 'here in the heart of the USA.'

'What, Puritanism and the religious subjection of women?'

'No, not that. I can't understand that at all, but they seem to reject the American culture of consumerism and waste. I can understand that.'

'I'll cut your hair with the kitchen scissors when we get back to the cabin.'

The rain had finally stopped by midday. We had lunch on the stoop and watched as Jen arrived in the battered pickup to prepare the next-door cabin for the big surprise. We called over to her in greeting and asked if there was anywhere good to eat in the town. She gave it a moment's thought and then gave us a blunt 'No'.

'Y'all will have to drive aways to Hopkinsville to find a

good restaurant. Try Aunt Mabel's on Turner Road. They do good food. Y'all have a nice evening now.'

Hopkinsville was farther than we thought, and the food was not good. The restaurant offered only the universal American fare of ribs, steaks and pizza. As usual, we were unable to eat more than half of what was brought to the table, and we left with styrofoam cartons of leftovers.

We drove back to our cabin and had just poured a glass of wine when a car pulled into the parking bay outside the next-door cabin. Our new neighbours had arrived. The car lights were turned off and doors opened and shut. We heard the trunk of the car shutting and eventually heard the next-door screen door squeal and slam. Then silence. My wife urged me to have a look, but I don't like curtain-twitching.

After another glass of wine I decided to attempt to light another camp fire in the firepit. I assembled the timber and newspaper in a cone-shaped pile and squirted on some barbeque starter. I applied a match and ignited the wigwam, which went off with a happy whoosh. Soon I had a nice fire going and my wife came out to join me with the rest of the wine. We sat in the humid darkness, lit only by the fire. We whispered. We conjectured about the nature of the surprise that was being delivered in the next cabin. Was it a surprise of passion, long withheld and suppressed by parenting? Were our neighbours tangled and throbbing on the clean sheets that Jen had so carefully stretched on the bed? Were they lying, sated and smoking, in the dark? Did the surprise go well? Was there a renewal, a recharging, a touching of the love-base, a reconnection? The fireflies danced like distant cigarette embers at a ghostly party. There were no lights and no sound from the neighbouring cabin.

We started to get sleepy around midnight and went to bed. We slept better that night, but both awoke sometime after three in the morning as we heard the sound of car doors slamming. A car revved and gravel ripped as tyres slipped, then gripped and pulled the car away. We slept again.

The dawn brought clear skies and sunshine in its wake. A beam of sunlight shimmied its way through the leaf canopy, through the cabin window and onto my face. It was a kind awakening, but bright. I folded back the covers carefully, not wanting to waken my wife, and padded from the bedroom to the living room to have a look at the day. It was then that I remembered being woken in the night. I opened the door of the cabin and stepped into the early morning, the boards cold and night-damp under my bare feet. There was no car outside the next-door cabin and no sign of life. I went back to the bedroom and slid into bed beside my wife and her warmth.

'Have they left?' Her voice was sleepy.

'There's no car there, and the cabin seems quiet.'

'They must have left when we heard the car last night. I wonder what happened?'

'A call from a babysitter? Some crisis at home?'

'Maybe she didn't like the surprise. Not sure I would.' She laughed. Her laughter caught the edges of my lifting mood and I laughed too. We laughed till tears came, and we lay, hoarse and gasping on the bed. Only she can do that to me.

As we slid back to sobriety, my wife said, 'Christ, I hope he hasn't done anything to her.'

I remembered the sound of the car tyres on the gravel – the hurried departure. What time had it been? I looked over at the deserted cabin.

'He could have buried her anywhere.' She wasn't smiling.

The thought was like a cold hand on my heart. I shuddered.

Later that day we checked out of Pine Ridge, packing our things and double-checking the cabin for forgotten possessions. We drove to the reception building to return the keys. Jim was standing in the middle of the yard. He was holding a shotgun. I slowed the car.

'Jesus Christ, he's got a gun!' said my wife.

I stopped a respectful distance away from Jim, not being sure what the gun was intended for.

'Christ, he's killed Jen and the little boy!' said my wife. 'He'll kill us too if we don't get out of here. Drive on, for God's sake!'

Then I saw Jen appear from the office building with a small boy in glasses holding her hand. Jim walked slowly towards the car, the shotgun held in his right hand, a cigarette dangling from his lip.

'Howdy,' he said, an approximate smile under his beard. He tucked in his shirt with his left hand.

'We're just checking out,' I said.

'No need for you to take the trouble to come up here. You could have left the keys in the cabin like the other couple,' Jen called, coming over to the car as well. My wife's imaginings of mass murder receded as she greeted Jen.

'Y'all have a nice day now,' said Jen, as we handed over the keys. In any other country the words would have sounded like a parody. Although she addressed us with natural Midwestern politeness, Jen seemed to be focusing her attention on Jim.

We turned the car and drove away. The sun shone on the puddles, and the woods glowed with a different colour of green from the day before. I felt my mood rise as I eased the car down the dirt road away from the doom-laden atmosphere of the log cabin. I glanced in the rear-view mirror and saw Jen and the little boy watching us leave, while Jim stood with his back to them, the shotgun in the crook of his arm. I banished the vignette and all thoughts of its potential tragedy as I swung the car out onto the open road.

A Missouri Break

It was Memorial Day, the last Monday in May, and we were driving along the banks of the Missouri river on the road trip of a lifetime. There were flags on every lawn, building and gas station. Sometimes there were two flags: one the Stars and Stripes, the other the Confederate Stars and Bars. The riverbank on our right rose in a tumult of vegetation towards the bluff high above us; the road snaked along, following the curves of the river to our left, and the river itself coiled and writhed in muddy flood, carrying occasional chunks of timber or whole trees in its course. The inexorable, unstoppable flow of the river was almost shocking; it moved at a pace faster than a horse could trot, endlessly and undeniably powerful, brown and primeval.

My wife and I had been on the road for three weeks and had already seen something of life in the Midwest. We had accepted that in this country the rich were very rich and the poor were poorer than we could have imagined in a land that prided itself on liberty, equality and democracy.

We had spent some time in Nashville and had toured the house built by President Andrew Jackson in the 1820s. We had seen where his slaves had lived and had heard that he was a relatively benign owner of humans. We noted the sense of embarrassment with which our white tour guide told us about the conditions under which the plantation workers lived and worked. As white people we shared some of that shame, and we wondered if things had changed much for the African Americans since they had been liberated to become the American underclass.

We had visited one of the famous honky-tonk bars on Main Street, Nashville, and had enjoyed some great country and rock 'n roll music. There is a fine, often non-existent line between country music and rock 'n roll, but it became very clear to us that country is for white folks. There were no black faces on the streets other than bouncers and beggars. We had not expected beggars.

The honky-tonks were all set up in a similar manner, with the band on the ground floor in what would have been a shop window, with their backs to the street. Often there was another band playing on the first floor, and sometimes yet another outfit playing on the second floor. There was no admission charge, but the beer cost five dollars a bottle, and patrons were expected to leave something by way of contribution for the band. Persons under twenty-one are not permitted to purchase alcohol in most states, and in Nashville, everyone entering a bar must show identification. This rule seemed to be applied in a haphazard manner, because we had wandered into several places without hindrance, until we met two bouncers at the door of one establishment. These gentlemen were both huge, even by American standards, squeezed and shoehorned into their black uniforms. They wore their hair cut aggressively short in the manner of trainee marines, and they had all sorts of badges and insignia on dog-tag chains around their necks. They wore headsets like Madonna wears when performing: a single earpiece and a throat-mic; an unseen supervisor was supervising and directing. Tucked away beneath the swell of their enormous bellies, they both wore belts on which hung all the paraphernalia of assault, restraint and death, including handcuffs, folding batons, what I took to be Tasers and, of course, handguns. Although it was night-time, both wore reflective dark glasses. One of these prodigies was black and the other was white, and they vied with each other for the role of 'bad cop'.

'Excuse me, sir. We'd be obliged if you would show us some ID.' Despite the ultra-polite language, this statement was delivered with a subliminal 'or else' attached. Both men held up their left hands as if ready to push us backwards into the street.

'I'm very sorry but we're visitors from Ireland and we didn't know that ID was required,' said my wife with a winning smile.

'Pardon me, ma'am?'

'We didn't know that we needed ID. We left our passports in the hotel.' She raised her voice in the way one does when a foreigner is having difficulty understanding English.

'I'm sorry, ma'am, but unless you have ID, you may not enter these premises.' He wasn't looking at us; his reflective sunglasses were scanning the night, watching for more people to bully.

'Look, we are obviously over twenty-one, aren't we? Surely you can allow us in?' I offered reasonably.

'Please step away from the door, sir!' This was delivered as a command. The 'sir' was tagging along to provide a veneer of respect to the otherwise naked aggression. The two gargantuan bellies were now advancing on us with a waddling sort of swagger, making it very plain in body language that we were to leave immediately or satisfy the two gentlemen's craving for violence.

'This is ridiculous!' My wife's hackles were up. 'Bloody Nazis,' she muttered, but discreetly.

'Step away, sir and madam!' There was real menace in his voice.

I thought of what might happen if one of these creatures were to actually lay hands on me. I would be crushed to death if one of them sat on me. There would be nothing left if both got in on the action. We backed obediently away. We left Tweedle Dumb and Tweedle Dumber to their victory and returned to the much nicer bar where they didn't seem to care who we were.

The band in this particular joint was good, and they were stompin' through their set. Folks were on their feet and dancing. There was a wide range of ages in the bar, from twenty-one to north of eighty, all mixing happily and enjoying the high-decibel, high-octane, country-rock vibe. The lead singer, a pony-tailed young man of about thirty, was using the bar as an extension of the stage, strutting up and down in his ragged jeans and his cowboy boots, his shirt loose and a baseball cap on his head, looking every inch a rebel against the establishment. At the end of each song he would jump down onto the barroom floor and take requests for songs – the accepted method of delivery being in writing on a twenty dollar note. He had just finished a particularly decent version of Lynyrd Skynyrd's 'Sweet Home Alabama', during which the whole bar had joined in, and had jumped down to the floor, when he was approached by a tall, burly man with a shaven head. They engaged in quite a long conversation while the band licked into an instrumental rendition of Springsteen's 'Born to Run'. The singer jumped up onto the bar again and sashayed back towards the band – with all the attitude that the patrons expected to see from a rock 'n roller of any calibre – exuding revolution and iconoclasm. When the instrumental finished he took up the microphone and thanked the audience for their patronage, then told us that the next song had been requested by Bob.

'Hey there, Bob, you know who you are!'

The tall man with the shaved head showed us that he was Bob by whooping and raising his hand in a fist.

'Well this is for Bob's daughter, Barbara, who leaves tomorrow morning with the armed forces bound for Afghanistan. We'd like to dedicate this to all the boys and girls who are serving with the forces and to their parents.'

The audience cheered till the bottles of Budweiser shook on the tables. The singer then said something to his band which we couldn't hear, and they launched into a solemn rendition of 'The Star-Spangled Banner'. The audience stood, hands on hearts, and sang the anthem together. Hats were removed and heads bowed. I felt the hairs rise on the back of my neck. I am not sure if it was reflected patriotism or fear. The united fervour was palpable. All differences were laid aside, and these people seemed ready to take up the arms that are so freely available and make war on anyone and anything that was perceived as a threat to the land of the free and the home of the brave. My belief that the USA's military involvement in the Middle East was a mistake that simply fomented hatred and terrorism was not a view that I would have aired at that moment. Any suggestion that the United States had no place in Afghanistan would likely have been regarded as a terrorist threat, punishable by death by lynch mob.

Next day, as we were having breakfast in our very expensive hotel, there was a loud explosion that shook the building. We hit the dirt, as they say in those parts, then felt foolish that we seemed to be the only people who had sought cover in this sensible way. A charming girl with an enchanting Tennessee accent explained that they were dynamiting to excavate the foundations for the building site on the next block and that explosions were detonated at nine and eleven every morning. All around us, unperturbed by the seismic rumble that had caused ripples in my coffee, the native patrons were feasting on stacks of pancakes with melted butter and maple syrup. It seemed to me that nothing would drive these people from the eating trough. The television screens – there was one everywhere you looked – were showing one of the all-pervasive advertisements for patent medicines that promised to make your diabetes better or delay its symptoms.

Now we were driving north along the Missouri, the mighty river that provided the gateway to the West and allowed the Europeans to expand their territories to the Rockies and beyond, driving the Native Americans before them towards virtual extermination. A huge sign on the roadside encouraged us to stop and eat at the Hawg Pit, just a mile down the road. The name intrigued us, and we pulled into the car park on the banks of the river. Most of the park was already taken up with what seemed to be hundreds of shining Harley Davidson motorbikes of all types and vintages. There were chunky tricycles, speedy-looking two-wheel roadsters and customised motorcycles with long front forks and tassels on every edge. Some of the bikes looked mean, others looked smooth; some looked like rock stars and a few looked like getaway machines. There were Sportsters, Tourers, Softtails, V-Rods and Dynas (I looked them up on the web), all polished and gleaming in the sun. Occasionally the air would be torn by the unbelievably aggressive farting roar of one of these machines as another customer arrived to join the fun.

We parked our hired Ford Focus in a discreet corner of the lot and made our way to the Hawg Pit itself. The side of the bar closest to the river was open to the elements, and there was a band of sorts playing rock 'n roll of sorts. A very tipsy middle-aged lady was dancing vigorously by herself. She was wearing very short cut-off jeans, a denim jacket proclaiming her membership of an illegible chapter of the Hell's Angels and a Confederate-flag bandana on her head. Her high-heeled cowboy boots were barely keeping up with her jive.

We ordered a beer and had a look at the menu. We were offered the universal American choice of hot dogs, ribs, steak or hamburgers. The thin-blooded could opt for a salad the size of a small vegetable market, with a choice of six different dressings, all of them fairly vile. I ordered ribs, to keep up appearances, and my wife ordered a cobb salad. While we waited for our food, we surveyed the crowded, noisy room.

I was expecting some bad-ass bikers: young and dangerous in studded leathers and torn T-shirts, extras from *Mad Max*, with long unwashed hair, bad manners and an evil attitude. But the crowd seemed to be in their fifties or older. The men, without exception, all sported the signature American pot belly, and some had their freshly shampooed, grey hair scraped back into a pigtail. The women wore stretch jeans, which were being put to the severest test, and denim shirts. Some of the men wore biker boots, which are large and clumpy, giving the wearer a cowboy gait. Others wore black motorcycle leathers and sleeveless denim jackets. The men showed a generous rear cleavage when they sat.

We were expecting a frisson of threat. We thought we might experience the thrill of eating in a bar on the wrong side of the tracks. We hoped that we would have tales to tell about pot-smoking, coke-snorting, amphetamine-crazed hoodlums riding around on their Harleys and terrorising the ordinary folks. But no. This had all the terror of a bank-holiday outing for retired accountants and their ladies. It just happened that they favoured Harley Davidson motorcycles as their weekend mode of transport.

Before we left, I visited the gentlemen's restroom. I was standing at the urinal, attending to my business, when I spotted a bumper sticker which a previous visitor had taken the trouble to affix to the wall at eye level. It was simple and direct. It was white, with a line drawing of a map of the USA in black, across which was printed 'Fuck Off. We're Full.'

Since then, they have elected Trump to be their president.

I'm not sure I'll be back.

The Father of the Bride

I wake at three in the morning. I dreamed that I was giving my speech and telling the joke about the two eggs that got married. This was vivid enough to put an end to sleep. I listen to my wife's steady breathing and think about her claims that she never sleeps. I listen to the silence of the deep night and wonder if the wedding is a good idea. Fairly soon I become convinced that, actually, it is a very bad idea, but there seems to be no way of unwinding it all at this stage. I consider the cost that might better have gone towards a deposit on a house for the couple as well as the wear and tear on me, my wife, my daughter and probably on the groom and his parents in turn. Just as I manage to doze off into a fitful nap, the clock radio comes on to jabber at me about the American nation staring in horror at the consequences of democracy. The red display shows 6.30. It is still dark and the big day has begun. I feel adrenalised butterflies stir in the base of my stomach and allow these to chase away the doom-laden mood of the earlier hours. I find myself humming 'Chapel of Love' as I shave.

On my own wedding morning thirty-five years ago, I fitted

a new Gillette blade into my 'safety' razor and accidentally inflicted several deep wounds to my jaw, which threatened to bleed out and put a stop to the proceedings (and to me). Small bits of cotton wool were stuck to my face as my best man drove me to the pub for a medicinal prenuptial gin and tonic. I looked like a scrofulous Santa Claus. In the men's jacks of that pub I prayed for fortitude and for effective clotting as I pulled the bloodied swabbing off. By some miracle the flow of blood had stopped. That was not the last miracle.

At seven o'clock, the hair-and-make-up lady arrives to primp and paint the bridesmaids who arrive shortly after her in their pyjamas. I find this touching. Some of these maids have known my daughter since they were four years old, but I'm fairly certain that they were not that alarming shade of orange back then. There are four maids in all, and they arrive in an assortment of shapes and sizes. And now they are all here, and all of them in perfect pitch. The make-up and hairdressing session resembles a prolonged girly haka in preparation for a Disney test match.

I skulk in the scullery, making sandwiches, whilst eavesdropping on the girly conversation, which is so inane that it manages to slither through my brain, leaving no trace or recollection of its contents. But the mood is undeniably happy and the happiness is infectious. I find myself whistling 'From the Candy Store on the Corner (To the Chapel on the Hill)'.

The forecast is for heavy prolonged showers giving way to incessant torrential downpours. By rights I should be building a large boat and organising the pairing off of animals. The bride reassures her bridesmaids that we have it all in hand

and that the 'Infant' is safely stowed in the hedge. The young ladies, being Protestant to a woman, seem bewildered as to why, if we had such a thing as an infant, we might be so cruel as to house it in the hedge. The make-up lady comes to the rescue with endless lore about the 'Infant of Prague'. Not being in any way superstitious, touch wood, my wife and I had listened carefully to all the lore about the Infant of Prague: a little, rather effeminate statuette of the very blond crowned infant Jesus, decked out in his sumptuous robes, orb in one hand and his other hand raised in blessing. He will, so the superstition goes, ensure a fine day for your wedding if you bury him in your garden or leave him in your hedge. It is said that he works best if his head has been knocked off accidentally. The bride and her mother had rushed off and purchased this little voodoo doll and had carefully stuffed him into the hedge the night before. And sure enough, the sun is shining. I think I have already mentioned miracles?

The autumn weather has been spectacularly kind. The trees are still decked in their dazzling end-of-season vestments, blazing in the sunshine. The oaks, across the valley from the back of our house, glow like two vast copper domes. The beech in our garden is aflame with autumn glory, and the maples and sycamores are vibrant yellow, gold and red. The ground is a tawny tapestry of ambers, golds and browns, constantly added to by new falling leaves. I have never seen it so vividly. It seems to me that the season has turned its volume up several notches especially for this day of all days. And now my own heart is dancing with joy for my little daughter, the bride.

For elevenses we open the Prosecco. As father of the

bride, I feel myself entitled to a little fortification. My wife returns from her local hairdresser looking lovely, and she joins us in a glass of wine. The girls are so happy and comfortable together that it is impossible not to laugh with them and become caught up in their enthusiasm for the day. I heat up the pastries and the full fry-up that I had cooked the night before. My two sons appear, devour all before them and then depart to join the groom. The mood is universally light and happy.

My lovely daughter retires with my wife to tog up. The other maids flit between the bedroom and the kitchen. By now the photographer and her female assistant have arrived, and the videographer has arrived also (he seems to need no assistance). Shots are taken of me eating a pastry, of the cat sitting on the railing of the deck and of the goldfish goggling from his tank. Then the photographic team are summoned upstairs to the bedroom. The videographer helps my wife to button up the back of the bride's dress. The finishing touches are applied to the hair, and at last I am finally summoned to view my little darling dressed as a bride.

Now, in spite of all my wife's injunctions, I have a little cry. It is my first sight of the dress, which had been commissioned nearly two years earlier and worth every penny of the vast sum paid for it. My daughter is so utterly beautiful, so radiant, so happy and so … herself. I am allowed a little hug but must take care not to smudge the make-up or disturb the hair.

Of course, by now my wife is dressed in her mother-of-the-bride outfit and has fixed her little hat on. She looks beautiful. She too is radiating happiness, although there is a residue of opening-night nerves, which are beginning to surface with constant references to her watch and requests for assistance in fastening her necklace and bracelet; her hands are trembling too much for the job.

Now we are in the wedding car. This is a deep loganberry-coloured 1952 Bentley. It's a real beauty – a proper conveyance to carry my wife, my daughter and me from our house to the chapel on the hill. The driver has all the cadaverous solemnity and unction of an undertaker. I think that driving wedding cars must be a sideline. He is wearing a fine, heavy Crombie overcoat from which his close-cropped bony head protrudes, tortoise-like. We set off for the church, taking a rather scenic route that is at once stunningly lovely and maddeningly exasperating because my wife and my daughter are by now beginning to fret about being altogether too late.

We arrive, and my wife goes in ahead of us. Final photos are taken in the car, then the great moment. I have loved my daughter since the day she was born. That love has grown into something so rich and powerful that it makes me giddy. Now I am struggling to avoid being overwhelmed by an ocean of love and joy. Tears are out of the question, although the eyes do mist a bit as we gather ourselves at the back of the church. We pause, then start our progress down the aisle as slowly as we can, drinking it all in. I find that if you walk too slowly, you tend to fall over. We moved just a hair's breadth faster than the falling-over point. There are the old friends, the dear relatives, the new in-laws and their friends; there are hats, the pastor, the groom and his entourage of groomsmen including my two sons looking dashing in their hired morning suits. I formally surrender my daughter to the groom, a boy I have known for eleven years, but still a boy. I rejoin my lovely wife.

The rehearsal had been a nightmare. We had assembled in the church at the appointed time and waited. The chosen celebrant – a kind, if rather otherworldly evangelical Christian pastor – had somehow managed to get lost despite meticulous directions and had run aground some twenty miles away. Phone calls were made and a search party comprising the groom's father and brother was dispatched. The pastor eventually found his way to the church but then we had to wait for the return of the search party. We looked to the gentle pastor for choreographical direction, but he just smiled a charming evangelical smile and suggested that we do whatever we liked. There were some tense exchanges that might have been looked upon as arguments between the protagonists with leadership qualities, of which there seemed to be a super abundance. The parish secretary, a no-nonsense Protestant lady, who had been extremely nice on the phone, started to go sour and took to polishing the brass of the altar rail with a vigour that suggested all was not to her liking. The groomsmen moved some heavy oak church furniture so that the principals might be able to fit at the altar. We were told rather crossly that this was all right as long as we left it back as we found it after the actual wedding. The rector, who had kindly agreed to the wedding taking place in his church, appeared briefly in plain clothes and, having been accidentally cut stone dead by both me and by my wife, retired again to the peace and tranquillity of the rectory. The palaver of the rehearsal took two hours and we were more confused afterwards than we had been before. Whether anything would turn out 'as we liked it ourselves' seemed extremely doubtful. Still, they say that it is good to have a bad dress rehearsal.

Now, on the day, our gentle lost-but-found-again pastor outdoes himself, delivering a profoundly spiritual and intimate service. The singer, a friend of the bride who is performing as a wedding present, sings like a gift-wrapped angel. Bride and groom announce their 'I do's' with loving conviction and are pronounced man and wife. The register is signed, and we leave the church to the strains of 'Signed Sealed Delivered, I'm Yours'.

The promised deluge is still holding off – the Infant-in-the-hedge is doing his stuff – which must be causing some puzzlement in meteorological circles. Photos are taken outside the lovely little church and then it is time to get in our cars and take to the road for the wedding venue, which is said to be about an hour away. I deliver my newly married daughter and her husband into the hands of the cadaverous tortoise and his magnificent car. I provide bride and groom with parcels of sandwiches (coronation chicken) and a large bath towel to prevent curry mayonnaise from getting on the wedding dress.

We have overlooked the early onset of rush-hour on Fridays, and we soon get caught in an exasperating creeping procession that would easily be outpaced by a Greenland glacier. It is like swimming through setting concrete. But my lovely wife and I are high on happiness, and we take the time to reflect on the day so far and to eat our own sandwiches, having taken care to spread tea towels like enormous bibs to keep our wedding garments clean.

There is nothing like a plan that comes together, particularly when the plan has been gestating for two years. We don't mind the rain that now torrents down, the Infant having finally given up the unequal struggle. Nor do we mind the darkness that seems to have gathered early. When we eventually arrive at the wedding venue, the avenue of beeches looks solemn and magical in the headlamps and fading autumn light. The house looks inviting and grand with lanterns on the steps and gentle lights in the windows. We sweep up to the entrance and step into the warm bustle of the house and its charming staff. Our car is parked for us, and our bags are taken to our sumptuous room that boasts a bathroom the size of your average ballroom and a bath that might have been used to train Olympic swimmers. Glasses of wine are put into my hand and forgotten on various ledges and tables; I hope with due regard for the French polish.

We pose for more photographs, and then we are called to dinner. The table plan was put together in record time by the bride and her mother. We tried to separate the ones that we knew would fight and to seat loud talkers on the deaf side of the acoustically challenged. I was pleased with the arrangements to the extent that I would have been happy to sit in at most of the tables; *noblesse oblige* calls me to the top table, where I have the groom's mother on one side and the gorgeous bride on the other.

The groom's handsome mother is a good talker, but with the notes for my father-of-the-bride speech burning in my pocket I find it hard to concentrate on her conversation. I sit transfixed and think of Coleridge's wedding guest, similarly caught by the Ancient Mariner. However, I like this woman, and she is warm and kind and fond of my daughter. I tell her how lovely she looks, and her stream of consciousness slowly dries up as she regards me with some gravity and asks me if I really think so. Yes, I do. Yes, she does. Everyone looks lovely today. Then the best man stands and calls the room to order for speeches.

I have been given my riding instructions: I am not allowed to cry; I am not allowed to humiliate the bride; I am not allowed to speak for more than forty-five minutes (sorry that should read 4.5 minutes) and I am not allowed to tell any of *those* jokes. What is left? I express my regret that those guests who have travelled specially to hear my famous run of honeymoon jokes are in for a disappointment.

I explain that my daughter was born with some superpowers, which include an ability, from the cradle, to slam doors and a knack of withdrawing all the oxygen from the room if she is not getting her own way. I recount a conversation when she was about thirteen:

'I'm going to a sleepover with friends from the Christian Youth Group.' This was delivered as a statement, not a question.

'Will there be a parent there?'

She shrugged.

'Do you have a phone number for the mum or dad?'

'For God's sake, Dad. This is *so* embarrassing.'

'Who else is going? I'd like to talk to some other parents.'

'EVERYONE is going.'

'Will there be boys and girls there?'

'Duh!'

'Well, you know that we don't allow you to go to mixed

sleepovers. You are teenagers, and things might happen.'

'For God's sake, Dad, they're all Christians!'

At this point all oxygen was removed from the room. Struggling for breath I tried, 'Where do you think that little Christians come from?'

Tears. Exit daughter, slamming door with such emphasis that the car alarm goes off and I lose several fillings.

In my speech, I now tell her how much I love her and that I think she is the most wonderful girl in the world. I encourage the groom to agree, because it will save a lot of silly argument later.

Then I turn to my own bride of thirty-five years, and now the prohibition on tears becomes something of an issue. You see, I married the girl I loved, and that love is still alive and kicking. I remember waiting for her at the altar, presented by my best man like a good soldier's rifle – smart, clean and lightly oiled. I remember being very, very nervous. I remember my heart leaping like a demented salmon with joy and happiness when she finally appeared, beautiful and radiant, at the back of the church on the arm of her dear father. She wrinkled her nose at me and I replied in kind. My married days have been one long honeymoon. In my speech, I now thank her for all this and feel that the words are inadequate, but the clock is against me.

I wish the bride and groom a thousand years of bliss, we drink to their health and happiness, I sit, and the room seems to swim around me.

The maid of honour, the groom and the best man all speak well. Everyone is nicely toasted and thanked. I want to hug the world.

We dance till four, swim in the bath and sleep like successful gladiators.

Perfect.

Acknowledgements

My patient wife, Clare, who endlessly listened and encouraged. My children, Amy, Guy and Hugh, for allowing me to write about them. Ferdia MacAnna, who took the cork out of the genie's bottle. Maria McGuinness, who edited with exceptional insight and wit.

Printed in Great Britain
by Amazon

70026268R00139